Namita Gokhale was born in Lucknow in 1956. Her first novel, *Paro: Dreams of Passion*, was published to widespread acclaim in 1984. Her other books include *A Himalayan Love Story* (1996), *Mountain Echoes* (1998), *The Book of Shadows* (1999) and *The Book of Shiva* (2001).

Namita Gokhale lives in Delhi with her two daughters.

Praise for Gods, Graves and Grandmother

'Gods, Graves and Grandmother *is remarkable on two counts. First, its structure of a modern fable held aloft by the gauziest of irony. And second, its searching scan of life in the downwardly mobile class of the Indian metropolises . . . Gokhale exposes the humorous underbelly of merchandized religiosity.*'

— India Today

'Gudiya's picaresque adventures cover a cross-section of Indian society . . . the novel is filled with people of all sizes and shapes . . . Like the Pied Piper, Gokhale has them marching to her tune.'

— The Statesman

'(Namita Gokhale) brings considerable literary maturity into achieving this tour de force.'

— Financial Express

'Set in the backdrop of semi-urban Delhi, the book effectively moves between the everyday details of poverty, ignorance and illiteracy and the supernatural realm of the temple which forms the focal point of Gudiya's life . . . A racy and engrossing book.'

— Sunday

Gods, Graves
and
Grandmother

Namita Gokhale

PENGUIN BOOKS

PENGUIN BOOKS

Published by the Penguin Group

Penguin Books India Pvt. Ltd, 11 Community Centre, Panchsheel Park, New Delhi 110 017, India

Penguin Group (USA) Inc., 375 Hudson Street, New York, New York 10014, USA

Penguin Group (Canada), 90 Eglinton Avenue East, Suite 700, Toronto, Ontario, M4P 2Y3, Canada (a division of Pearson Penguin Canada Inc.)

Penguin Books Ltd, 80 Strand, London WC2R 0RL, England

Penguin Ireland, 25 St Stephen's Green, Dublin 2, Ireland (a division of Penguin Books Ltd)

Penguin Group (Australia), 250 Camberwell Road, Camberwell, Victoria 3124, Australia (a division of Pearson Australia Group Pty Ltd)

Penguin Group (NZ), 67 Apollo Drive, Rosedale, North Shore 0632, New Zealand (a division of Pearson New Zealand Ltd)

Penguin Group (South Africa) (Pty) Ltd, 24 Sturdee Avenue, Rosebank, Johannesburg 2196, South Africa

Penguin Books Ltd, Registered Offices: 80 Strand, London WC2R 0RL, England

First published by Rupa & Co 1994
This revised edition published by Penguin Books India 2001

Copyright © Namita Gokhale 1996, 2001

12 11 10 9 8 7 6

ISBN 9780141006994

This is a work of fiction. Names, characters, places and incidents are either the ~~product of the author's imagination~~ or are used fictitiously, and any resemblance ~~to actual persons~~ or locales is entirely coincidental.

The India Club, Inc.
books@indiaclub.com
BOOKS · PAINTINGS · CD ROMS · MUSIC

d Singapore only

Typeset in Sabon by Mantra ~~Virtual~~ Services, New Delhi
Printed at Repro India Ltd., Navi Mumbai

AUTHOR'S NOTE

I am convinced that every novel has its own horoscope, its special kundali, an observation with which Pandit Kailash Shastry would certainly concur. *Gods, Graves and Grandmother* was written in 1992, when I was recovering from a serious illness. It was completely unlike my first novel, *Paro: Dreams of Passion*, and met with a somewhat puzzled reaction. David Davidar of Penguin had first encouraged me to write it, but it is only now, several years later, that he is publishing it. Jatin Das was to design the cover for the first edition, but could not; his son Siddharth has brought it to life this time.

Some changes have written themselves in in this new edition, but the story still inhabits a long-ago time which could very well be today. Suspend disbelief if you must when you read this book, but not belief.

ONE

awkward English

When my mother went away, my grandmother and I were left to fend for ourselves. I had always been given to believe that we had once been enormously rich, but at that time we were on the very verge of penury. We would indeed have starved had not my resourceful grandmother stolen a marble slab from the building site behind our shanty. This marble—clean, cold and veined with the merest hint of green shadows—she placed beneath the holy peepul tree which shaded our little hut. Then she found five rounded river stones, purloined them, really, from a sahib's rockery, and arranged them on the marble altar. Marigold flowers from the sahib's garden, and the third stainless steel thali which we didn't need, now that mother had gone, and our shrine was complete.

Grandmother extracted a ten rupee note from the folds of her withered but still substantial breasts, and we walked together to the tea shop at the end of the road. She ordered a cup of tea, which I was instructed to drink. I felt grand and important sitting in a chair with a table before me.

I ordered a biscuit from Shambhu, the Bihari giant who owned the tea stall. Shambhu had a mass of flesh where his left eye used to be, and I was convinced that he was a dacoit on the run from the police. I even felt a certain affectionate complicity on this score.

Grandmother didn't object to my ordering the biscuit (it wasn't really a biscuit but a nankhatai) and when I was finished, she paid the bill and we returned to our hut. She extracted the change we had collected from Shambhu out of the voluminous drapes of her sari bodice and placed it ceremoniously upon the stainless steel plate which had been mother's. Then she prostrated herself before the pebbles and the marigolds on the green marble slab, lay down so still and silent and for so long that I was afraid she might be dead or in a coma.

'Are you all right, Ammi?' I whispered in her ear. By then the eyes she possessed in the back of her head had alerted her to the presence of a passer-by, and a garbled chant, distinctly pious and devotional, emanated from her trained singer's throat.

In the evening we lit an earthen lamp at the shrine and performed aarti. Shambhu of the tea stall produced a large luminous conch shell from which he coaxed an awesome and angry wail. Two strangers stopped by on their way home from office. They clapped and kept time as grandmother clanged the brass bell that had magically materialized and now hung like some mystical fruit from the branches of the peepul tree. I was still a stranger to the paraphernalia of religion, brought up as I had been, ignorant of God or Divinity, and I puzzled to make sense of the unfamiliar tableau as the flickering lamp cast new shadows on my grandmother's trusted face.

After everybody had left, we put the change from the stainless steel thali back into a pouch and locked it in the tin trunk, which was the only furniture we possessed besides our two charpoys.

The next morning the notes and coins were back in the thali. As I was returning from my ablutions from behind the building site, I heard the clink of metal on metal and miraculously there was more money on the plate than there had been when I left. A man in a helmet, clutching a briefcase in his folded hands, was standing beneath the peepul tree, his head bowed in prayer. You could say that we were in business after that. *interesting even though she said she wasn't into God*

Sacred to Lord Shiva, the peepul tree was a presence in our lives. Its leaves talked to me in a sibilant murmur, and I knew that ghosts and spirits dwelt in its enormous gnarled branches. At night I was sure I could hear them, laughing and talking in a perfectly normal way. Sometimes they would scream—soft, strangled sounds that only I could hear, which would make the hair on my arms stand up on end and send a shiver down my spine.

My grandmother, never well-versed in the higher tenets of Hinduism, knew enough about practical folklore to warn me about disembodied souls that flocked to the murmuring branches of the sacred tree, waiting only to pounce into the mouths of unwary travellers and take possession of them. She made me take a solemn oath never to yawn under the peepul tree, or open my mouth in any way, without first snapping my fingers to scare away these phantoms.

Then, to assuage my fears, grandmother pointed out that these spirits were helping us, actually serving us, that they were in a sense our familiars. It was the shrine beneath the peepul tree that kept us fed and clothed, although we were of course not as rich as we had once been, very long ago.

Money poured in: eight annas, five rupee coins, even the occasional fifty rupee note. The miracles were not yet manifest, but we were already rich beyond our wildest dreams. We had no neighbours to discredit us, and as the tea-shop wallah also shared in our sudden prosperity, having diversified into the sale of coconuts and marigold garlands, we faced no scepticism from that quarter. So must it have been in the first heady days of Mecca.

TWO

[handwritten margin notes: • fairy-tale sentence structure • non-concrete view of time]

But to begin at the beginning. Before mother left, in a long-ago time, we had been very rich. There was a big house, a haveli with a hundred-and-thirty rooms. Besides twenty-two servants, these hundred-and-thirty rooms were occupied by my mother, my grandmother and my grandmother's younger brother, whom my grandmother had brought up as her own son.

My grandmother had been a great singer, a kothewali whose voice was more liquid and beautiful than Lata Mangeshkar's. Eleven nawabs and two Englishmen were besotted with her. Carriages, buggies, Rolls Royces and Daimlers used to line up outside the house in the evening. Perfume from the flowering mogra and chameli spilled out into the street, and if a man were to innocently walk past that house, when he got home his wife or mistress would sniff suspiciously and ask where he had been.

My grandmother's younger brother, my mother's Mamaji, grew up in a distant wing of the haveli, and was kept protected, even innocent, of the gaiety and abandon of those feminine evenings. Mamaji had studied in the best schools and colleges, and was destined to redeem the family. Although he was only a few years younger than my mother, they hated and despised each other.

I confess I cannot really remember actually seeing my Mamaji. Memories can be quite confusing. Sometimes they run in slow motion or are jerky and abrupt like an old black-and-white film. My memories of my childhood are marked by a sort of sepia tone, like the photographs in a very old album. There were actually some old photographs in the bottom of the tin trunk, but Ammi tore them up and threw them away. I still carry the torn edges of many of these memories, but they merge into each other, they do not match.

One of the things that I can remember perfectly well is the design of a large carpet. It is a blue carpet, with a pattern of leaves and flowers woven in reds and pinks. The pink leaves puzzle me; I wonder why they are not green. My memories are inhabited by such contradictions. There is an image in my mind of a peek-dan, an elaborate brass spittoon, into which my grandmother, a diamond flashing on her fine nose, would squish out chewed-up betel-nut juice with unerring aim. I can also recall a silver hookah with a long curving nozzle; I remember listening contentedly to its soft gurgling, but I cannot conjure up the face or figure of the man who is smoking it. Then I remember the mango tree in the courtyard, the one on which my Mamaji hung himself. A hard green mango fell on my head once. I had a bump on my head and I wept relentlessly. My mother tried to console me, and promised to make it into a special sweet-sour pickle, which of course she did not. My mother was not one to honour promises.

Then something very bad happened; nobody ever told me what. I know that my Mamaji died. He was found hanging from the mango tree in the shady courtyard with the raat-ki-rani and chameli bushes. Somebody else died too, someone my mother always referred to as 'Him'. In the long late mornings, when my mother and grandmother thought I was asleep, they discussed 'Him' in tragic whispers. 'He' died, and the police got suspicious.

The customers stopped coming. Policemen, bailiffs, lawyers, grocers and pawnbrokers took over our beautiful house. My mother went bald with worry. Her long frizzy blonde hair began falling out in fistfuls, and lay scattered about, glistening on the velvet bolsters in the baithak. Even her eyelashes and eyebrows began falling out. Grandmother took her to all the famed vaids, hakims and quack doctors of our town. On their prescriptions, grandmother massaged Bhringaraja taila on her scalp. It smelt foul and aggravated the problem all the more.

We went to Lucknow to consult a famous Ayurvedic doctor. He charged a hundred rupees as fees, and advised us to powder and incinerate the right tusk of a male elephant, and apply it, mixed with ghee and honey, overnight for two months.

The tusk was on offer for three hundred rupees. Grandmother brought him down to two-hundred-and-fifty; but it was no use. The potion only irritated mother's skin, and angry red spots began appearing on her scalp.

My grandmother pawned her silver hookah to buy mother an imported American-style blonde wig. She sold the horse and buggy in which they used to visit nearby towns for marriages and mujras. The harmonium player proposed marriage to my mother. She consented, but they were both afraid of my grandmother and decided to elope. They left in a hired tonga, at the crack of dawn, but he gave her the slip at the railway station and decamped with her luggage and her jewellery. She waited there for two days, watching out for him from the Ladies Waiting Room, certain that he would return.

When she walked back home on the third day, my Ammi would not allow her back. It was only on my intercession, for grandmother never denied me anything, that the maidservant opened the double latch on the front door and let her in. All her fine clothes had disappeared. She looked different, even more defeated than before. Grandmother refused to lend her anything, but finally she relented and gave her an old burka, which my mother wore with nothing on underneath when she occasionally washed the clothes she had run away in.

Then there was the court case. I believe it created a sensation when 'His' wife attacked my mother in the corridor outside the courtroom. The two women wrestled and grappled on the floor. There was no one to cheer my mother on. That woman tore through mother's burka, then seized her blonde locks and threw the wig out of the window. My mother took the witness box without her hair, her fair glistening skull more embarrassingly naked and sordid than the sad accusations against her. We lost the case and everything we had.

We left the haveli at the crack of dawn, as the birds chirped and the morning haze floated around the town. I can still remember the smell of the chillum the tonga driver put away, the aroma of horse and tobacco, the kind eyes of the old nag, kinder than any I had encountered for a long time.

Then to many houses in many towns, but never for long. One night in Bhusawal, as we were changing trains, my mother sighted her harmonium player. She began shaking and twitching like a peepul tree at midnight, but she didn't tell grandmother until the train he boarded had steamed out of the station. Grandmother never wasted her time on anger. She took a betel nut out of her paan-daan and cracked it with her silver saropa. 'I'll do that to his skull one day,' she promised mother.

Without her hair, mother was no longer any good for trade. We had nothing to fall back on. Grandmother improvised a makeshift wig, with black cotton parandis and a pink and gold trim, but it was quite hopeless. At the Jhansi railway station, grandmother befriended an old beggar. He had a white beard and wise eyes and looked like a dervish. 'Come to Delhi,' he told her. 'It's a city with a future. A lot can be done in Delhi.'

And so it came to pass that, dusty, dispirited, and desperate, we arrived in the capital of India. Riyasuddin Rizvi, for that was the name of the ancient beggar, was a gentleman. He too had seen better days and his conversation was laden with oblique references to an aristocratic past. He showed me a tattered photograph of a beautiful woman with long eyelashes and a sad smile, which he kept in his wallet.

'I can't tell you anything about her,' he said with a mysterious nod, leaving me to devise a time-consuming and very satisfying game about the sad lady's identity.

Rizvi Sahib took us under his wing. When we arrived at the Old Delhi railway station, he hired an autorickshaw for us, not a tonga. Grandmother pointed out the sights of Delhi. 'That's the Red Fort, Jahanpanah Jehangir ruled from here,' or 'That's the Old Fort, Humayun fell down those stairs on his way to the library.' Riyasuddin Rizvi nudged me on the elbow. He smelt of damp and vomit. 'Your grandmother is a learned lady,' he said. 'I hope you grow up the same.'

We stopped on a lonely stretch of road, far from the noise and bustle of the city. Riyasuddin Rizvi extracted a maroon leather pouch from the depths of his achkan and kurta. He presented this with some ceremony to my grandmother, who accepted it graciously. 'Allah gives, and Allah takes away,' he said simply, and the autorickshaw sputtered off into the sunset.

Grandmother and I sat down in the shade of a peepul tree to count the money, while mother kept a lookout for thieves and strangers. The pouch contained nine-hundred-and-eighty rupees. Six hundred were in crisp new banknotes, and the rest in crumpled rupee notes and small change. Grandmother pondered over the money for a while and counted it again. 'A pickpocket,' she pronounced finally. 'Let us check our own trunks.'

Mother rummaged through the piles of embroidered shawls, sequined ghararas and beaded reticules that were the sum total of our worldly possessions. A violent blush suffused her face, crimson on white, and I realized that my mother was an exceptionally beautiful woman, even though she was, for the moment, bald.

THREE

non linear story

To return to the peepul tree. After mother left, after she ran away with Riyasuddin Rizvi, less than a week after we had counted out the money, grandmother grasped that we had to diversify to survive. Although we had no neighbours on that lonely road except Shambhu from the tea stall, a slumlord, one Sundar Pahalwan, exercised territorial rights over the stretch of pavement. He arrived at our hut one morning. I can still remember the sight of his bulging bodybuilder's frame as it blocked out the light of the dim Delhi dawn. Our straw and brick jhuggi did not yet have a door, and even the cow-dung plaster on the walls had not completely dried.

'Ten rupees a week,' he said, sharpening the edge of his moustache, 'to be revised after two years. If that is not acceptable, the girl can beg on the crossroads, thirty per cent to our syndicate. If the girl is inclined, you could beg, and she could occupy herself better . . .' His eyebrows arched in innuendo, and an incongruous, utterly charming dimple appeared under the thick stubble.

Grandmother had abandoned her burka the day we arrived and consigned it to her trunk, along with the sequined ghararas and beaded reticules. Now she assumed an entirely different persona.

'Arre Rama, Rama, Rama,' she exclaimed, her honeyed voice taking on a new texture altogether. 'Seize our money, Pahalwanji, but spare our self-respect. I am the widow of a Brahmin, my husband was a priest, guard your tongue or else a virtuous woman's curses may follow you!'

Sunder Pahalwan was taken aback. 'Come on, out with the cash!' he said. His tone was already uncertain.

'If you come here this same time next week, I will have it ready,' grandmother replied, dabbing at her eyes with the corner of her faded cotton sari.

When Sunder Pahalwan returned the following Monday evening, a raggedy crowd of worshippers were already assembled around our shrine. A gold and red gharara from our trunk had been restructured to form a glittering canopy. A statue of Durga astride a tiger was lit up by an electric bulb which a religious-minded lineman had connected to the street lamp. Grandmother's voice, her perfect, liquid voice, fulfilled the gloaming evening sadness. She did not fumble with the words or stumble with the verses. She was word perfect, as well she might be, having practised the bhajan late into the night, with only the whispering peepul tree for accompaniment.

After Sunder Pahalwan had gone, leaving eleven rupees on mother's thali, and the milkman had left us a litre of milk in an earthen container and Shambhu had touched Ammi's feet and sought her blessings, I summoned up the courage to ask grandmother the questions which were puzzling me.

'How did you know those songs, Ammi? Where did you learn them?' I asked, clutching her white dhoti and nestling in her lap, for I was missing my mother.

'In my mother's lap,' she replied, 'in her lap, just as you are sitting in mine. Arre, Gudiya, these religions, what should I tell you, they are a type of fashion. Bombay cut, Calcutta style, London look. In the old havelis, the fashion was for Moghul beauties from Persia, from Samarkand. And so, being a fashionable lady, my mother switched to burkas. Here, now, under this peepul tree, perhaps this is better. In foreign countries, England, Amreeka, Christ is the fashion, so those phirangi women, they wear skirts and even trousers. Don't trouble yourself about all this, or your hair will begin to fall out like your mother's.'

I drank up the warm smelly buffalo milk and drifted off to sleep. I never questioned her again. Our temple grew in fame and fortune. Shambhu from the tea stall became our trusted lieutenant. When the man from the Municipal Corporation came with a demolition order for the pucca cement structure which now housed us, he fell at grandmother's feet and begged her forgiveness for the blasphemy.

'What does the department know of the ways of God?' he asked, and left a fifty rupee note in the donation box we had installed. Soon his boss, a bald man in a three-piece suit, arrived with a copy of the demolition order. The light which the electrician bhakta had illicitly taken from the street lamp via an overhead wire exploded on the departmental chief's head, burning his nose to a melted bulbous stump. He was rushed to the dispensary for first-aid. His wife and his mother visited us the next morning. They left five hundred rupees, a sari and a shawl for grandmother, and their profound apologies.

The electrician got a promotion. Shambhu found a wallet full of cash in the bench outside his tea stall. A scorpion bit a man who spat in the direction of our temple. Everyone knew that the Will of God was guiding us. We felt invincible, all of us, in our separate ways.

It was decided by grandmother and Shambhu that I should be given an education. I had been exposed to an itinerant schooling, in the form of one nursery and one municipal school. Now I was dispatched to the nearest scholastic institution. The St. Jude's Academy for the Socially Handicapped, run by an obscure charity, was considered 'as good as a mission school'. I was admitted, at the age of eleven, to the second grade.

Needless to say, I was the tallest child in my class, but the fact that I lived in the temple near the peepul tree with a grandmother who was the local godwoman gave me a certain aura.

The girls at school were envious of my skin, the pale-gold skin some Afghan forebear or ferangi customer had endowed me with. The teachers saw that colour as a sign of redemption.

It was an existence fraught with conflict. Did not my mother's burka languish in our tin trunk? Having deposited me in school, grandmother took no further interest in the matter. I attended St. Jude's in a casual sort of way, coming and going much as I pleased.

Yet the temple was my home. My grandmother, in her new avataar, was no help in resolving these contradictions.

The principal of St. Jude's was a pale Parsi lady with gentle eyes that hid behind thick spectacles and the kindest face I had ever known. Roxanne Lamba took an immediate fancy for me and singled me out for her attentions.

Shambhu too was impressed by my new learning. He would make me recite the alphabet to him. 'A for Apple, B for Ball, C for Cat,' I would go, rushing like a locomotive all the way to Xylophone, Yacht and Zebra, though I had only the faintest notion of what these objects actually were. Shambhu would look on proudly, and when I was through he would reward me with a nankhatai or a biscuit.

My grandmother considered it all a waste of time. 'I have seen a lot of learned men,' she would say, scrunching up her face in distaste. 'Their minds get dizzy from too much thinking. I remember your Mamaji...' Her voice dropping to a whisper, her old eyes glistening with the suggestion of tears, she stopped for a moment to look like the Ammi I knew.

'You're better off learning to cook, Gudiya,' she said, regaining control again. 'Become a good cook and marry a respectable man.'

We didn't have a kitchen. The cooking was done on an open three-brick choolha, fuelled by cowpats which some devout lady bhaktas supplied us with. Grandmother was not much of a cook; it was a skill she had never cultivated and we survived primarily on the fruits and mithai the bhaktas brought to the temple in great quantity.

There was no mirror in the temple, nor was there one in Shambhu's tea stall. I had consequently little or no idea of what I looked like, although I could see that my hands and feet were very fair, and my unkempt hair was a peculiar brown colour, bleached further by the sun. Sometimes I would catch my reflection in a polished steel thali and practise a dazzling smile, for I was, even then, a vain child.

Sometimes grandmother would get down to combing my hair. Complaining about her eyesight, she would extract the nits, one by one, and squash them dead on a stone. 'Your no-good mother ran off to have fun!' she would mutter, 'after all, bringing up a young girl is no Gudiya-ka-khel.'

Although I was all of eleven I had never possessed a doll. 'Buy me a doll, Ammi, please,' I would wheedle, 'a golden-haired doll that can blink and move its arms.'

Although she indulged me in every other way, this was a matter about which grandmother was strangely adamant. 'Chhi chhi chhi!' she would expostulate, 'What would you do with a golden-haired doll? You're a good girl!'

'What do good girls play with, Ammi?' I would enquire earnestly. 'Why can't they play with golden-haired dolls? And why did you name me Gudiya?'

Grandmother knew how not to reply to questions. She unbent enough to instruct Shambhu to buy me a kitchen-set, but the minuscule pots and pans did not interest me in the least, although they were the only toys I had. To this day I do not know why she denied me a doll. Perhaps she considered it somehow idolatrous.

FOUR

The open field behind the tea stall and the peepul tree where Riyasuddin had deposited grandmother, mother and me had been dug up to make way for Janata flats which the government was constructing for indigent sections of society. Labourers from central India had swarmed to the site and were proving a godsend to our burgeoning temple finances.

Making provisions for tribal tastes, Shambhu allowed a young Bhilala boy to distil a mahua type of country liquor in the open sewer behind his tea stall. The tribal women, with their silver jewellery, flaring nostrils and breasts straining with strength and sensuality, were completely uninhibited personalities, and a rather wild mood prevailed in the untidy cluster of huts near the construction site.

Soon Magoo, one of the younger women in the site, succumbed to Shambhu's charms. Shambhu too seemed irrevocably infatuated. They were always together at the tea stall, smiling into each other's eyes, although Shambhu of course had only one.

Grandmother grumbled that Shambhu was behaving like

an old fool. Magoo's husband, Saboo, would spend all his time sulking outside the tea stall; only he didn't drink tea but country liquor from the stall behind the sewer. Shambhu began talking about marrying Magoo.

One night Magoo's enraged husband hacked off her head with an axe. He dragged her corpse to the thicket behind the temple and buried her there. Then he set off in search of Shambhu, whom he located sitting in the temple in conference with my grandmother.

Grandmother saw the look in Saboo's eyes and understood the situation at once. Shambhu was too preoccupied to notice anything. Ignoring grandmother's urgent eye-signals, he yawned elaborately and left.

Grandmother set about calming Saboo. She gave him a glass of cow's milk, warmed and sweetened, and talked to him soothingly of maya and illusion and how the world was just a dream within a dream. My grandmother had a well-acquired knowledge of how to handle men, and by the time Saboo left he too was caught up in the beautiful world of non-importance, of nothing matters, God's will and Allah's inayat.

Sometimes when I am tired and weary, I simply return to that time and moment, lying in my grandmother's lap, with the world just an illusion, something to be tolerated, something easy that passes like a hot June afternoon before the cool of midnight and the smells of fragrant night-flowers engulf and embrace us.

Magoo's husband left the blood-spattered axe behind and disappeared into the cool night, headed in fact for the shack behind Shambhu's tea stall where the narangi liquor was brewed. After fortifying himself, he made for Shambhu's room and tapped softly on the door. Foolish Shambhu opened it. His visitor knocked him down and dragged him to the bushes behind the peepul tree. There he smashed a rock upon his head and killed him. Then he returned to the temple, breathing heavily.

'I've come for the axe,' he told my grandmother. No words of reason could penetrate his anger, which was a palpable thing, like a cloud of bees buzzing around his head. Grandmother tried to stop him with subterfuge and sweet words and yet another glass of warm milk.

Saboo was not to be pacified. 'I am from Alirajpur,' he said, his tongue thick with liquor. 'Once upon a time we were mighty warriors. Now they call us criminals. But we can still kill for our honour!'

He staggered out, still brandishing the axe. Then Ammi left too, leaving me alone in the spooky courtyard with its flickering shadows and decaying marigold smells. I was not used to being by myself in the temple; grandmother was always there. Even inside our room, I felt I was being observed from all sides by the enormous staring eyes of the gods and goddesses. I hated the sensation. Trembling with fear, I crept out of the room into the dark night. Stationing myself behind the peepul tree, from which I could see Ammi's huddled figure out of the corner of my eye, I settled down to my silent vigil.

Saboo was digging furiously in the thicket, spraying mud and bush in all directions, whistling softly to himself as he worked. He excavated deeper and deeper until he was tired, panting, sweating. He was no longer whistling. The Ekadashi moon shone upon Shambhu's sprawled-out body, and I remember wondering how he had fallen asleep in such a peculiar position. He must be asleep, I decided, and then trained my eyes on my grandmother, still and sentient as a hooded snake. Saboo was very angry. He was swearing, foul and filthy words poured from his mouth as metal hit metal and a lumpy bag sprang out of Shambhu's grave and threw a shower of gold at grandmother's feet.

Saboo was so involved in the burial that he did not even notice the gold. One-eyed Shambhu slumbered on, his eternal sleep not disturbed by the violent kick with which Magoo's husband dispatched him to the grave. Grandmother was motionless as a little mongoose in that snake-infested dump. I knew that she had noticed me, that the eyes she possessed in the back of her head had already alerted her to my presence beneath the peepul tree. As Saboo began shovelling the earth back over Shambhu, grandmother seized the moment and scurried forward to pick up the glimmering gold coins that lay scattered around her feet.

Soon the sound of soft sibilant snoring rose and fell from Shambhu's grave. Saboo was asleep. Grandmother motioned to me, and I could hear the crackle of twigs underfoot as I tiptoed over to her. We gathered the gold coins and put them in the bag. She sent me back to the temple for a candle, and we scoured every inch of ground before us by its flickering light. But there was no more gold.

We crept back home. Grandmother bolted the door, and we spread out the treasure before us. There were thirty-two gold sovereigns, heavy, shining and weighted with the power of wealth.

'Hai Allah,' grandmother exclaimed, forgetting for the moment that she was a pious Brahmin widow. 'Hai Allah, beti, these are gold asharfis from Emperor Jehangir's time.'

She put the thirty-two gold coins back into the oilcloth pouch, which she wrapped in an old petticoat. Our treasure vanished into the trunk, and as she snapped it shut I saw the sequinned chunnis and glittering ghararas hidden there and I was reminded of my mother and my Mamaji and that long-ago haveli which had once been our home.

It was that strange season, that hiatus between summer and the monsoon, when not a leaf stirs, and the nights are heavy with stillness and expectation. Then suddenly the air trembles and the thunderstorm awakens like a hundred maddened furies and beats the leaves out of the trees and the crows out of their nests and the dust rises in spirals like spirits from their graves.

When the storm broke, my ever-talkative peepul tree grew almost demented with excitement. It flapped its arms and writhed in a sinuous stormdance. Even though my expectant eyes were shut tight in denial, I could still see the ghouls and evil spirits that cavorted on its branches. They bared their teeth and grinned and beckoned to me to join them.

High on the upper branches I could glimpse Shambhu and Magoo, naked, hidden by the leaves, leering at me as they performed obscene and unspeakable acts. I tried to close my eyes, but they were closed already and I could not shut out the vision. And then again, in those branches, suspended against gravity, I saw my sad beautiful mother, and she too was naked and she too was enjoined in the unspeakable act with Riyasuddin the beggar.

I was sweating with terror and a fearful excitement had invaded my nether regions. I wanted to see exactly what it was that they were doing but the frenzied clapping of the leaves as they whispered and whistled feverishly to each other obscured them and prevented me from a clearer knowledge.

I opened my eyes to find grandmother looking at me concernedly. I pretended to fall asleep again. She unbolted the door and very quietly left the room. I could see that it was almost morning, a faint streak of light heralded the day. That comforted me, and I got up and opened the tin trunk under my grandmother's bed. The coins were cold and heavy and unlike anything I had ever held. I took out one gold guinea and hid it in the secret pocket my Ammijan had stitched into my undershirt. 'This is Emperor Jehangir's gold,' I told myself once, and then again. The peepul tree was still shrieking at me, but I ignored it and fell into the heaviest sleep of my life.

FIVE

When my life changed again, I was not at all surprised. Just when the soothing rhythms of the tabla and the tanpura had become the accustomed backdrop of my childhood, there came the clatter of the tonga which hurried my mother to the railway station with the perfidious harmonium player. When I had begun to accept my grandmother's new avataar and our life together at the temple as somehow quite normal, Shambhu's stupid passion for thick-lipped Magoo led to my grandmother's arrest for suspected homicide.

Yet so much had happened to me in my short life that I simply did not respond to grandmother's arrest or her subsequent release and vindication. Fear, sorrow, surprise or any kind of reaction completely failed me. Even memory abandoned me, and it is only from hearsay that I can patch together an account of what happened.

When Saboo awoke after burying Shambhu, he returned to our temple courtyard and begged forgiveness of grandmother and the assembled deities for his hideous crime. He handed the blood-spattered axe to grandmother and begged her to decapitate him. When she refused, he left the axe before the statue of Kali that we had recently acquired, thanks to the patronage of a Bengali devotee and returned to his job on the building site.

Shambhu was reported missing, and then the two bodies were unearthed. My poor, clever grandmother knew nothing of the forensic sciences, and when the police found the axe and her fingerprints on it, she denied everything and anything, denied for that matter even knowing Shambhu or Saboo or Magoo. She sat me on her lap and maintained a stubborn suspicious silence, her prayer beads in her hand and a murderous scowl on her beautiful ravaged face. Deft as she was at the art of survival, she knew that some terrible and unplanned retribution had finally overtaken her.

There were many people, such as the official upon whom the light bulb had exploded, or Sundar Pahalwan the street-lord, whom my wily grandmother had sometimes foiled, who rose in arms against her. The electrician, the milkman and a few others rallied in her support. The rossogulla vendor, who had donated the statue of Kali, maintained his neutrality, but the wife and the mother of the official from the Municipal Corporation were staunchly with grandmother.

Add to these the numbers of the merely curious, and we had almost a hundred people crowding around the temple all day for no less than a month. The tin collection plates were overflowing, but grandmother wouldn't touch them. Shambhu had been in charge of the money, but now he was dead. None of the other bhaktas seemed to know what to do or how to handle my Ammi. She would sit silently in the courtyard with her prayer beads, her ferocious scowl igniting her whole being into a Kali-like picture of wrath.

Of course the police were very careful not to play up the powerful passions which the case had excited. They took her to the thana only for a day, and most respectfully, with five lady-officers as escort. I can never forget the look she gave me as she left, the stubborn resistance to the world's outrage which her eyes conveyed to me, taught me. When at last she returned from the police station she was her old matter-of-fact self again, she went about her chores with her usual swift economy of movement, emptying out the collection boxes, sorting out the notes and the change from the withered flowers, and storing them in the new steel trunk she sent the electrician to purchase. She even gave me a glass of warm milk to drink and removed the nits from my hair.

Meanwhile, all kinds of fantastic stories and rumours began circulating, none of them as improbable as the real story of her life. It was whispered that she was a hundred years old, that she knew magical spells that could change the sex of an unborn baby, that she had ordered the execution of Shambhu and Magoo as part of a ritual sacrifice.

The police arrested Saboo. After three days in the lock-up, he was affected by violent remorse and made a long and emotional confession in which he completely exonerated my grandmother of any knowledge or complicity in the murder. He went on record to state that she was a most holy woman who had tried to reason with him, had, in fact, even given him a glass of warm cow's milk to drink, to calm him down and dissuade him from murdering Shambhu.

The legal process, once initiated, transported him from

the police lock-up to judicial custody and thence to the portals of the Tihar Jail. He was given seven-and-half years for culpable homicide not amounting to murder, in view of the grave and sudden provocation of Magoo's inexplicable love for one-eyed Shambhu. He was to emerge from Tihar Jail fourteen long years later, but that is another story in another time and another life.

Shambhu was dead. His wife came to Delhi for the inquest and the funeral. After it was all over, she decided to stay on. Phoolwati was a plump and attractive woman with the most enormous bosom possible. She had a commanding personality and possessed a better head for business than Shambhu had ever displayed. Although she had never previously left her village in District Madhubani, Bihar, she knew precisely what she was about, and before we knew it she had negotiated a reduced five-year rental from the street-lord Sundar Pahalwan, with a percentage of the take thrown in.

The tea shop was expanded, the moonshine business divested, although it had never belonged to Shambhu in the first place. Phoolwati set up another stall just outside the temple which sold incense and marigold garlands and coconuts and little brass amulets which she had ordered from Moradabad. One afternoon Phoolwati came to visit grandmother, accompanied by a photographer. Grandmother was flattered, her woman's vanity and innate coquetry resurfaced, and she obligingly posed for the camera. Within a fortnight, colour postcards of my grandmother, with 'Om' printed across them in gold-embossed lettering, were for sale outside the temple for two rupees each.

My grandmother began to believe in God. She took to fasting four days a week. Even when she was not fasting, she would eat just fruits and nuts and sometimes a little yogurt. She took a vow of silence, and remained completely mute for a month, crouched silently in a corner of the temple, her stubborn eyes resisting any questions or answers or any kind of communication with anyone. She stopped combing my hair or looking out for nits or feeding me or plying me with warm milk. She was not unkind, but she withdrew into some intense and personal confrontation with the statues and idols around her; often I would find her muttering queries to Durga or Hanuman.

A luminous peace began to float like a cloud over her, distancing her from me. I learnt to stand on my own feet and even began to look after grandmother in a fumbling, uncertain way. Sometimes I would comb her hair, or coax her to eat some rice and curds. Her skin became incandescent and an electric energy seemed to light up her still presence. The money continued to pour in.

I noticed that Ammi's mouth would often fall slackly in a way that looked stupid, even senile. Yet the expression in her cataract-clouded eyes was rapt and beatific. Soon she began ignoring me altogether, concentrating solely on her prayer beads or else singing hymns and bhajans in a startlingly strong and youthful voice. She had, as I mentioned, almost stopped eating altogether. She had become thin as a stick and a smell compounded of the essence of old age and sandalwood incense enveloped her.

As for me, my grandmother's neglect hurt me deeply. I felt fundamentally betrayed and was actually jealous of those impostors, those new-found gods and goddesses, who had stolen my grandmother from me. I conscientiously committed acts of minor sacrilege, forever looking for newer and more ingenious ways of provoking their holier-than-me presences to declare their rivalry. I would pull faces at them or pluck flowers after sunset or deliberately wear my school-shoes within the temple precincts. But nothing I did managed to aggravate them, and their serene painted faces remained as pious and distant as ever.

Nobody bothered with me, and I was left to fend for myself, which I learnt to do rather well. I went to school as I pleased, ate what was available, observed everything I could.

I had outgrown all my clothes. My salwars reached to my calves and my kurtas were little more than shirts. I was growing taller every day, and an awkward grace was making itself manifest. My naturally fair skin was tanned a pale brown, and my hair bleached to a strange near-blonde colour from too much playing in the sun.

'Your hair is almost the same colour as hers,' Ammi said to me once, with a sense of deep foreboding. I shuddered in delicious anticipation; there was nothing I wanted more than to be like my wicked waylaid mother.

Every night, as I fell asleep on my folding cot near the window, the peepul tree would begin its seductive song. Shutting my eyes tight against the visions, I would still encounter the energetic acrobatics of Shambhu and Magoo, of my mother and Riyasuddin Rizvi. There were other ghouls and spirits who dwelt in that peepul tree, a man with a blank featureless face, no eyes or nose, nothing save a large red mouth that was always laughing. And then a sad polite lady who was always sighing and who smiled apologetically whenever she caught my eye. Except for my mother and her friend, and Shambhu and Magoo, none of them ever mocked or frightened me; they had indeed over the years become my beloved and trusted familiars.

SIX

In spite of her distraction, grandmother administered the temple with an iron hand. Everything had to be perfect. The premises were kept scrupulously clean, and all the devotees who constituted the 'inner circle', the little band of believers who had surrendered themselves to Ammi's wisdom, had specific chores assigned to them. There was somebody to sweep the courtyard, to polish the brass and silver, tend the flowers, mind the chappals, count the change, keep track of the holy days, distribute the prasadam and attend to all the other seemingly unimportant details that constitute the daily life of a temple.

After Shambhu's death, the task of handling the cash had devolved upon his widow, Phoolwati. There were those who, presuming upon grandmother's otherworldliness, tried to fiddle with the accounts or take home an offertory of ghee or sweetmeats. They were always rudely surprised by the extent of grandmother's administrative control and by the range and vigour of her vocabulary as she rebuked them for their misdemeanours. Word spread about Ammi's extraordinary ability to sense out miscreants, adding to the already considerable accretion of myth and mystery that surrounded her.

An old woman with a single yellowed tooth which strayed out of her mouth like a minuscule tusk had attached herself with a peculiar ferocity to my grandmother. I always thought of her as being very, very old, though in all probability she was much younger than my Ammi, and could not in fact have been any older than fifty-five. Yet there was a droop to her body, to her voice, to the defeated tilt of her shoulders that spoke of awesome and immeasurable age.

This old lady, who was named Lila, had wandered into an evening aarti, accompanied by her son, who was a clerk in the local ration shop. Grandmother was in particularly fine form that week, and her bhajans seemed to reach out to some distant and lonely spot in the minds and hearts of her listeners. Lila sat enthralled by Ammi's singing, and when it was all over and everybody was leaving, fumbling for their chappals and sandals by the gate, she continued to sit in the temple courtyard, rooted to the floor as if she was, as Phoolwati later spitefully remarked, a pile of cow dung.

Something about Lila aroused Phoolwati's instant hostility. She referred to her as 'that buddhi' or 'Ekdanti', in honour of her single protruding tooth. Lila took Phoolwati's hostility in her stride and cheerfully accepted the major burden of the temple workload. No task was too difficult or demeaning for her, and she attacked all her chores with the same unexacting enthusiasm. She washed grandmother's clothes, and mine as well, and meticulously ironed them with a cantankerous cast-off steam-iron she had purchased from the local dhobi.

Lila used to water the tulsi plant in the temple courtyard everyday except Sundays. One Sunday, imitating her example, I took a brass pitcher of sacred Ganga water from the temple storeroom and ceremoniously poured it over the holy tulsi plant in the courtyard. This show of piety was actually quite uncharacteristic. If I remember right, I was more than anything inspired by Hema Malini in the film *Sholay*, and dimly connected the worship of the holy basil plant with the propitiation of certain heavenly forces that were empowered to someday grant me a handsome and virile husband.

When Lila saw me watering the plant, she got very upset. She grabbed me by the shoulders and shook me violently. 'How dare you!' she snapped, 'don't you realize that it's Sunday, you little jungli?'

'So what?' I protested, startled by her sudden belligerence. 'After all, I'm only watering the tulsi! What can be wrong with that?'

My innocent query was met by a stinging slap across the cheek. Some incomprehensible trigger had transformed Lila into a tigress.

'You live in a temple and ask me such questions?' she roared, and led me by the ears to my Ammi for chastisement.

Ammi was equally bemused by her tirade, but being Ammi she did not let on to what she did not know. 'Arre, Lila, our Gudiya is still a child,' she said expansively, 'and the shastras allow to a child many follies that are forbidden to grown-ups. Surely you understand that?'

Lila let go of my ears and murmured an apology, not to

me but to my grandmother. My young vanity had never been so rudely violated. When Phoolwati heard about the incident, she energetically fuelled further discord by suggesting that Ekdanti was jealous of my privileged relationship with my grandmother.

'Arre Gudiya,' Phoolwati snorted. 'I know this kind of woman! I know what she wants! That old one-tooth just can't abide peace! It's always complain, confuse, destroy!'

The quarrel escalated into a full-fledged feud. Lila remained conspicuous by Ammi's side, pressing her legs, solicitously massaging the soles of her feet. Phoolwati would murmur 'Ekdanti, Ekdanti' under her breath, wherever and whenever she saw Lila. Lila remained serenely oblivious to her detractors. She stopped washing my clothes, which I rather regretted. Apart from that she betrayed no further signs or symptoms of the remarkable anger which my watering of the tulsi on a Sunday had aroused in her.

Grandmother began to depend increasingly upon Lila, who attended to her every personal need. Of course Phoolwati remained her trusted lieutenant, and no major decision in the temple was ever taken without her, but Lila had insidiously succeeded in rendering herself indispensable. For one thing, she was always available, having all but abandoned her son and his family. Grandmother had only to cough or look around vaguely, and Lila would materialize like an obliging djinn to attend to her every unspoken wish.

Phoolwati resolved that the time had finally come to rid the temple of Ekdanti. She enlisted the help of Lila's son and daughter-in-law, persuading them that their mother had moved into the temple compound only because she felt spurned by her family.

'Arre, beta, try to understand a mother's heart,' she exclaimed virtuously. 'She is pining for the love of her son and his wife. It is the greatness of our Mataji that she lets Lila stay on here with us, but her weeping and wailing is really upsetting everybody! After all, this is a temple. All of us who are living here have left our worldly ties far behind!' With that, she fixed an unblinking stare upon Lila's son, the clerk at the ration shop, until he was shamed into promising that he would take his mother back without delay.

awkward english

After the lamps had been lit and the evening bhajans were over, Lila's family confronted her. Her son and daughter-in-law had come along with her grandchildren, and together they prevailed upon her to return home.

Lila looked imploringly at grandmother, but she was feeling inward again and had retreated into a private reverie. The rest of the assembly took an active interest in the unfolding family drama. The majority of the devotees were of the view that Lila was best off with her own family and counselled her to heed her son and return to his household. Lila listened patiently, and then, still saying nothing, rose to her feet and meekly agreed to follow her family home.

Phoolwati's triumph was short-lived, for the very next day Lila returned and could be seen imperturbably continuing with the task of massaging the soles of grandmother's feet.

Then came the miracle of the bananas. After Phoolwati's arrival in Delhi she had in her rustic way planted innumerable banana and papaya trees around the temple compound. They grew at an incredible speed, rushing up to meet my knees, my waist, my pigtails, until soon they stood silhouetted tall against the blue Delhi sky. However, although they multiplied, they were not fruitful. Young banana saplings would sprout up overnight beside the mother plants, and move at the same incredible speed from adolescence to maturity, but there were no signs of any bananas. Phoolwati took this as an affront to her own personal powers of propagation. Lila further compounded matters by observing in her most guileless manner that fruit trees planted by barren women, especially barren widows, could never prosper.

This remark was not made directly to Phoolwati, but temple politics being what it was, it was conveyed to her with the utmost dispatch.

Phoolwati's fury knew no bounds. Her childlessness, which she blamed entirely upon Shambhu's absence from District Madhubani, was, she insisted, only yet another proof of her shining virtue. Who was Lila to talk about the virtues of motherhood in this Kalyug when matriarchs abandoned their domestic duties to wallow in the comforts of temple life? Had she, Phoolwati, been blessed with children, had that philandering Shambhu performed his conjugal duties, she would never have abandoned her offspring!

Lila maintained her composure and continued to attend to Ammi's needs. To her roster of duties she now added the zealous care of the fruit trees Phoolwati had planted.

Grandmother appeared to be completely ignorant of these developments and so managed to maintain her neutrality. In one of her evening discourses she rambled on about male trees and female trees, masculine bananas and feminine papayas and the balance and harmony of nature, of Shiv and Shakti. 'Even the holy peepul tree can be bound in matrimony to a young bough of the margosa,' she explicated. 'Such is the nature of life.'

Phoolwati, who normally never paid much attention to her discourses, became violently agitated. Her breasts began to heave with emotion and she was convulsed by such an exaggerated attack of acidity that her belches could be heard punctuating grandmother's theorizing about the male and female principle.

The next morning we awoke to a strange sight. Clusters of ripe yellow fruit had miraculously materialized on Phoolwati's banana trees. They clung to the smooth green stems with joyous fecundity. Phoolwati herself was busy harvesting the crop, rushing from bough to bough, bunches of bananas draped over her enormous bosom like primeval adornments.

Lila watched silently, her placid face betraying no signs of scepticism. Perhaps she was more subtle than I had imagined.

Suddenly an army of chattering monkeys materialized, seemingly out of nowhere. A large and athletic primate bounded energetically into the compound, followed by another and yet another. In a few moments they had stripped the banana trees bare and soon the grounds were littered with banana skins. An exceptionally bold monkey even attacked Phoolwati and attempted to make off with the bananas draped across her chest, but she repulsed him with a fierce cry.

Lila's simple face wore an expression of ecstasy. Her tooth waggled and shook in an absolute epiphany of joy. She ran into the temple and emerged with a brass platter containing a ghee lamp and an incense stick.

'Jai ho!' Lila exclaimed rapturously. 'Hanuman ji ki jai!' So saying she began scattering handfuls of uncooked rice on the departing posteriors of our visitors.

The two women embraced each other. I wondered if Lila's tooth was making its presence felt in the region of Phoolwati's abundant cleavage. The remaining bananas were distributed among the devotees, and grandmother was promptly alerted to the miracle of the monkeys.

'And it's a Tuesday!' Lila kept exclaiming. 'Hanumanji himself chose to visit us and eat those godsent bananas on a Tuesday!'

'Jungle mein Mangal,' Phoolwati said good naturedly, and peace was established between grandmother's two acolytes.

SEVEN

Grandmother judiciously refrained from remarking on the miracle of the monkeys. This disappointed Phoolwati, but she consoled herself for having at least vindicated herself and was content to leave it at that.

Ever since Riyasuddin Rizvi had decamped with my mother, grandmother had developed an extreme aversion for beggars and all forms of beggary. When, one day, a trio of lepers stationed themselves at the temple gates, their tin cans positioned besides them and their stubby arms spread in supplication, grandmother threw a fit. She bound her sari pallav tightly around her waist in a pert manner uncharacteristic of her present avataar, flounced out of the temple courtyard and accosted the three hunched figures.

Ammi gave full vent to her displeasure, displaying a vocabulary of such extreme vigour that Lila and Phoolwati, who had followed her out, looked at each other in wonderment. The lepers, for their part, were immune to invective and stared at her mutely with their gentle beseeching eyes.

When she saw me standing beside Phoolwati, she finally lost control. Something seemed to have snapped within her. 'Send them away!' she screamed, brandishing a twig she had picked up. 'They don't deserve to sit before the house of God!'

One of the beggars took out a flute and polished it with his maimed hands. Holding it to his lips he coaxed out a tender melody. I stared in fascination at his disfigured face, transfixed now by the pure notes of the bamboo flute.

'Forgive us, Mataji, all we ask of the Almighty is that he may grant you peace of mind,' he said meekly. His mouth was red with pan and his teeth stained with nicotine.

'I do not require your intercession with the Almighty,' grandmother said tetchily. 'If you are on such good terms with him I suggest you ask him for a motor car and a bungalow! Whatever you do, move your backside out of my temple premises.'

The lepers were as obdurate as she was. They clambered on to their small makeshift tin skateboards and propelled themselves a little way away, positioning their warped bodies under the shade of a spreading mango tree.

'The road belongs to the government, the tree belongs to God,' the one who had been playing the flute said in an oracular voice. 'May the Almighty grant you peace of mind, mother.'

Grandmother hobbled back to her room, trying unsuccessfully to control her rage. Lila started massaging her feet, and Phoolwati took me away to her hut to braid my hair with a new red ribbon which she had bought for me from the Thursday street market.

The next day Sundar Pahalwan arrived to intercede for the beggars. 'We can get a good income from them!' he said seriously, after prostrating himself with suitable humility before grandmother. 'You must keep in mind, Mataji, that most temples do allow these unfortunates to take up residence outside their gates. They get their alms, the visitors get their blessings. It's all fair and above board. If Phoolwati sells a garland for seventy-five paise, the remaining twenty-five will find its way to them. You don't lose, I don't lose, they don't lose. What's the harm?'

Grandmother didn't deign to reply and assiduously maintained one of her famous silences. Sundar sat around, waiting for her response. 'Well, keep it in mind, Mataji,' he said at last and left. Phoolwati followed him out.

After the evening aarti, grandmother held forth on the subject. 'Something for nothing is against the laws of karma,' she said. 'We all have to strive, to make an effort. These beggars are like middlemen who want to intercede between you and your gods. They are pimps, dalals. Never give your hard-earned money to them!'

One earnest member of the congregation raised his hand. 'But Mataji,' he said 'are not Brahmins and pandits also a type of middleman? Don't they also intercede between man and his gods? I am a bania, a shopkeeper. Why should I pay a commission? I can pray directly to Goddess Lakshmi!'

Grandmother waved his question away impatiently. 'Arre, beta,' she replied, 'we Brahmins and pandits are not beggars! We are giving you something in exchange. We speak for you, we speak for God. It is like hiring a lawyer or an advocate! Where would you be without us?'

The shopkeeper was not convinced and began framing another long-winded question. Lila spun into action, and sidling up beside him, urged him to be silent and not waste grandmother's time with his silly queries.

Grandmother sat back quietly, a mystical smile hovering upon her face. I wasn't convinced by her arguments. If, in their piety, the devotees could support us, why should they not extend their support and sympathy to the three lepers? I wanted to discuss this with Ammi, but she would give me no opportunity to engage her in conversation. She rarely talked to me now, and there was in her manner towards me a detachment and disengagement which kept me from her. I missed my mother desperately and decided that it had been my grandmother with her stone heart who had driven her away.

I voiced my views to Phoolwati. 'I think she was unkind and unfair to those lepers,' I said. 'Why should she grudge them a few rupees?'

Phoolwati agreed with me wholeheartedly. 'I disobeyed your Ammi today!' she exclaimed. 'I gave those poor creatures a few rupees and some old laddoos! That Bhurroo—the one who plays the flute—he is really very talented. He could have been a great musician! Whatever your Ammi may say, my mother always taught me to give alms to the poor! But promise me, Gudiya, that you won't tell your Ammi what I did.'

EIGHT

One day a police car drew up outside the temple, flanked by two outriders and a motorcycle. An important looking man in a police-officer's uniform strode out, followed by a weepy, tired looking memsahib who had to be all but carried in by the attendant constables.

Grandmother was sitting in the courtyard, getting her feet massaged by Lila. The woman collapsed at grandmother's feet in a dramatic and somehow insincere way. Lila gave her a murderous look. The police officer sneered sceptically at us. The lady began sobbing dramatically. Phoolwati brought her a glass of water, which she drained to the last drop. In between her frenzied weeping, grandmother managed to coax the following story out of her.

The memsahib's husband, Kalp Nath Sinha, was a high-ranking police officer posted in Ghaziabad. Their teenage son, who lived in Delhi with his grandparents, had crashed his motorcycle and suffered a cerebral haemorrhage. He had been in a coma for three weeks now, and the doctors had told the family to give up all hope. The boy's grandmother, Mrs Sinha's mother, had dreamt that an old woman who lived in a temple would be able to cure him. They had scoured all the temples around Delhi and met several old women in several temples, but to no avail.

Now that she had seen grandmother, Mrs Sinha was convinced that their search was over. Ammi was the old woman ordained to bring her son back to life.

Lila was extremely moved by the story. 'Our Mataji will heal him!' she said joyfully. 'Surely you have come to the right place, beti!'

Ammi looked irritable. Her jaw trembled and a little ball of spit formed in the corner of her mouth. I was afraid that she might slap Lila, but instead she addressed the weeping mother in the gentlest of voices.

'When exactly did the boy's grandmother have this dream?' she asked carefully.

Mrs Sinha told her. The police officer was observing the scene ironically. His eyes had the hard look I had noticed in other policemen at other times.

Grandmother was silent for a while. She scratched her head and wiggled her finger in her ears, and looked puzzled and confused. My Ammi was always so dignified in her person and carriage that it disturbed me to see her so. I couldn't understand why she was being so crude and fidgety.

Then grandmother addressed the policeman. 'Come back at the same time, next week,' she said to him. 'Make sure you bring your mother-in-law with you.'

A little crowd of acolytes gathered around us, eager to witness a miracle. Phoolwati was prominent amongst them. Now, as the police officer and his wife returned to their vehicle, she rushed after them, panting with exertion.

'Take these!' she shouted, thrusting a photograph of grandmother and a silver amulet into the police officer's hand, 'and put them under your son's pillow tonight.'

They departed amidst the screech of police sirens, leaving a pall of diesel fumes upon the beggars seated under the mango tree.

Grandmother retreated into her room and did not appear for the evening bhajan. The next day she was very withdrawn and refrained from communicating with any of us. Even Lila was barred from entering her room. So it remained for a week, although Phoolwati managed to persuade her into making an appearance for the evening bhajans.

A week passed, and then ten days, but the policeman and his wife did not reappear. One day a taxi drew up, and Mrs Sinha alighted, accompanied by an old lady wearing dark glasses. Mrs Sinha was radiant, there was a spring to her step, and she looked quite unlike the shattered woman we had last encountered. Phoolwati led them eagerly to grandmother.

Grandmother examined them quizzically. An expectant silence sat over the room, each party waiting for the other to speak. It was grandmother who broke the silence.

'Well, is he better now?' she asked cautiously.

Mrs Sinha once again proceeded to collapse at grandmother's feet. The old lady took off her dark glasses and declared that it was indeed my Ammi who had appeared in her dream. Both Lila and Phoolwati preened about and looked self-congratulatory, but grandmother silenced them with a grim movement of her hand.

'Is he better now?' she asked, sucking in her lips into an odd grimace as she spoke.

'Yes,' Mrs Sinha replied. 'Yes, my son is much better. A specialist is flying in from London tomorrow and the doctors say we mustn't lose hope.'

'But you must lose hope!' grandmother replied. 'If there is anything in the world you must lose, it is hope!'

'You mean my son will die!' Mrs Sinha exclaimed. Her mother looked devastated. Her old woman's head began wobbling uncontrollably upon her ancient neck, like some ridiculous toy. She was old and decrepit, with sagging yellow skin. A smell of decay hung over her. I realized anew how beautiful my Ammi was.

Phoolwati's bosom was rolling and heaving, as it always did in moments of agitation. All of us in the room were caught up in the drama. Only Lila remained calm, her usual look of extreme placidity plastered over her face.

Grandmother ignored all of them, and walking over to a corner of the room, extracted a needle and a thread from a rusty cigarette tin in which she kept her odds and ends. She took a faded cotton sari which was hanging from a peg on the wall and began mending it with conspicuous and uncharacteristic concentration. She kept on stitching for a very long time, much longer than was rationally required for the little tear on the sari pallav. Phoolwati's chest stopped heaving, and, losing interest, she returned to her shop to preside over the marigold garlands and incense sticks. The police officer's ancient mother-in-law calmed down, rubbed her eyes and once again put on her dark glasses. Mrs Sinha settled herself on the floor and waited resignedly for grandmother's attention. Lila continued to smile abstractedly.

An hour later, grandmother was still at her mending. Her sewing was jagged and untidy. She kept jabbing the needle into the fabric and out again. I was certain that she would hurt herself. At last she put the cloth away and looked tenderly at Mrs Sinha.

'He will be all right again,' she said, 'but only if you can persuade your husband to desist from a certain activity. I am sure you will understand what I mean.'

Mrs Sinha blushed painfully and then she started weeping anew. Grandmother signalled them away, and Lila rose to her feet and ushered them out.

After that, we had no news of them for a very long time. Phoolwati, eager to announce a new miracle, tried very hard to find out more, but to no avail.

One afternoon a police jeep drew up, and a familiar looking police officer strode out and marched purposefully towards grandmother's room. But grandmother was busy, she was meditating, or thinking about something, or perhaps she was just sitting vacantly, letting the past and the present jumble in her mind with all the strange obscure thoughts she seemed always to be entertaining.

Mr Kalp Nath Sinha waited for a while, glancing repeatedly and impatiently at his watch. Then, with a muttered exclamation which could have been a swear word, he began walking back to his jeep. Phoolwati confronted him excitedly.

'Is he better?' she exclaimed, 'Is your son all right now, inspector sahib?' Her face was wreathed in an expectant smile.

'Yes, he is all right now,' he snapped, and moved away. His constables surfaced and cordoned him protectively.

'And where is Mrs Sinha?' Phoolwati panted, as she ran after him.

'She has gone away,' he replied, as he got into the jeep. He slammed the door shut and disappeared to the shrieking of sirens.

Phoolwati was disappointed and outraged. As a miracle, it was not much to build upon, for there had been no resolution of the tension. The resurrection lacked the elements of drama and glory she so constantly craved.

Of course, she was not the one to give up, and she began working assiduously on the incident, giving it, in retrospect, the dramatic integrity which it lacked.

Later I heard her recount the story to a visitor. It was an altogether more satisfactory version of events, with moral and allegorical overtones. Soon the story spread, and as is usual with these things, improved further in the telling.

Despite grandmother's disavowals, the inevitable spate of seekers surfaced. Every morning Phoolwati would eagerly escort in an assortment of accident victims, convalescents, and chronic hypochondriacs. Grandmother's vigorous rebuttals and disclaimers regarding her healing powers made the believers even more certain that they were in the right hands. The legend spread that she could heal with a look. Ammi had to resort to holding morning darshans, where the faithful swarmed in, armed with marigolds, coconuts, and incense, much to Phoolwati's satisfaction.

NINE

The three lepers had established themselves under the mango tree. They had constructed a small shed the size of a chicken coop by the side of the road. Their skateboards were parked neatly by the pavement and their tin cans were always placed on precisely the same spot. They were methodical about everything they did, and had gentle, pleasant manners. I asked if they were brothers, but they said no, they were only friends.

The flautist, Bhurroo, never went anywhere. Rain or shine, he remained seated calmly under the mango tree. Phoolwati had a soft corner for him. Braving grandmother's disapproval, she spent long hours chatting with him. Their conversations were usually one-sided, for Bhurroo never ventured to say anything, but constantly obliged Phoolwati by agreeing with her every remark.

The feud between Phoolwati and Lila had been only partly resolved, with each demarcating her duties and territory. Lila was the official keeper of the 'Panchang', the Hindu almanac, and, being better informed about the ways and vagaries of Vedic ritual, was elected to keep grandmother informed about impending auspicious and inauspicious dates, and the observances thereof. Grandmother always brushed off her subtle pressures about keeping the monsoon chaturmas fast or offering milk to snakes on Nagpanchami or not washing her hair on Thursdays, but this never deterred Lila.

'I quite understand, your holy grandmother is beyond these kind of ceremonies,' she would mutter, her single tooth shaking sagaciously. 'I shall undertake the fasts on her behalf. After all, I'm only an ordinary mortal, paap and punya still apply to me!'

One day Lila looked up from her Panchang to announce that there was to be a total lunar eclipse. It was an unlucky conjunction. Upon no condition would she allow any of us to walk around outdoors that night. As for the idols and holy presences in the temple, they were to be completely cordoned off to ensure that the evil aspect of Rahu as he swallowed up the moon did not contaminate or defile them.

Grandmother treated this outburst with a benignly indifferent smile. However Phoolwati, who demanded a constant and unrelenting pace of activity, was tremendously taken by the idea.

'Yes, and the next day everyone can offer coconuts and a garland of marigolds to Hanumanji,' she said.

'Whatever for?' I asked.

'That nothing bad happened to them during the eclipse, of course,' Phoolwati replied impatiently.

'But suppose something bad does happen?' I persisted.

'Of course it won't, how can it, with your grandmother around?' she retorted, with irrefutable logic.

Grandmother glowered at her.

'Well, actually,' Lila said self-importantly, 'if one were to follow the shastras, the correct procedure is to offer a kilo of raw urad ki dal and a length of black cloth to a beggar, to propitiate Rahu. I thought everybody knew that!'

I could see that the very mention of beggars had irked Ammi beyond measure, but she restrained herself. During her evening discourse, grandmother surprised all of us by obligingly mentioning the eclipse. She requested her devotees to maintain the ritual injunctions and stay indoors for the duration of the moon's banishment. Lila crept up to the dais and whispered something in her ear. 'And especially pregnant ladies,' she added, 'or otherwise there is the danger of a deformity. Rahu's influence can penetrate even to the womb!'

That evening all of us hurried through our routines. Phoolwati returned home early, and Lila retired to the room behind the temple which had been allotted to her. I crept into bed, keeping out of grandmother's way, as I had now learnt to do, to avoid her frequent and inexplicable rages.

Grandmother seemed unusually relaxed that evening. She caught me gazing at her and gave me a mischievous smile, the kind I associated with long ago, when we had been rich.

I stared at her in surprise as she opened the door and walked out into the dark.

'But Ammi,' I said fearfully. 'Tonight is the night of the eclipse!'

'I know, Gudiya,' she replied gaily, 'and that's why there isn't any Phoolwati or Lila around to pester me!'

Together we tiptoed out into the black night. The temple looked very different, there was nobody about, and the devi-devtas seemed restless and watchful. We skirted the main building and crept noiselessly towards the shrine dedicated to the nine planets, the navagrahas. Grandmother settled down on a pile of rubble. There was a rustle of something that may have been lizards, or even snakes, but I was not at all afraid, for I was alone with my grandmother at last.

Suddenly there was a great flapping of wings. Birds began crying out in many tongues. The shrill calls of crows, koels, parrots, mynahs and kestrels tore at the inky night. A swarm of mosquitoes was buzzing about my arms, but there was something about the quality of the night that impelled me to be still, and I did not even bother to scratch at the mosquito bites.

Grandmother was humming to herself. It was a happy lilting melody. She stroked my hair gently, as she had used to, and I thrilled with pleasure at being touched by her again.

The faint ripple of a flute answered her song. It was the beggar Bhurroo under the mango tree. I looked up anxiously, worried that her mood might change, but she seemed not to have ever noticed.

'When I was your age, Gudiya,' she said, still stroking my hair, 'I wanted to be a film star. There were only silent films in those days, no sound. I wanted to be like Zubaida or Jayshree. But look at me now—a holy woman! Truly, no one can understand the ways of God!'

She was turning pensive again, and I was afraid that the renewed intimacy between us might suddenly snap. I looked up at the moon. The faintest suspicion of a shadow was beginning to crawl about its surface—a tiny black spot that grew bigger and bigger. The birds were getting more excited every second, and their shrill ear-splitting cacophony made it impossible to even hear what Ammi was saying.

I couldn't read the expression on her face. Tentatively, I touched her cheek. She continued to stroke my hair. Suddenly she got up and pulled me to my feet. Enveloped by the black night, we returned to the temple.

Lila was waiting for us there. She was in a terrible state of agitation; she didn't know where we had been; her intuition had warned her that something was wrong; how could we have been so rash as to leave the room?

'It's all right, Lila,' grandmother replied soothingly, without a trace of irritation. 'I have many siddhis, and these things do not have the power to affect me.'

This pacified Lila somewhat, but she insisted that I was to immediately bathe with some Ganga water she had stored for just such a contingency. It was essential to cleanse oneself after being exposed to an eclipse. 'After all, these rituals do have some meaning,' she muttered angrily to herself.

She carried in a lota of water from her room and stood in stern supervision as I threw it over myself. The floor was a mess, and I had to mop it up after I was through.

The next day Lila gave the beggars under the mango tree a packet of rice, a kilo of black urad dal and a length of black cloth. When grandmother came to know of it she grunted cynically, but she did not say anything. Lila and Phoolwati took this as a sign of acceptance, and thereafter the trio of lepers were gradually integrated into the life of the temple.

TEN

One night I awoke to the sound of grandmother fumbling about in our dark incense-lit room, her arthritic fingers struggling with the rusting lock of the old tin trunk. It hadn't been opened for almost a year now, ever since that fateful night when Saboo had burst into our sanctuary with murder in his eyes. Finally, the key moved in the old Harrison lock and grandmother carefully extracted the oilskin pouch with the gold coins and hid it under the pallav of her sari. She slipped out of the room, silent as a whisper.

Once again I slipped out after her. It was Poornamashi, and the full moon hung suspended complacently over the still slumscape and the tired fields, imparting a repose and dignity to the struggling lives and the sparse and sorry vegetation. Silvery light irradiated the peepul tree and the stagnant monsoon pond behind it. Grandmother had evidently planned ahead, for a small pit had been excavated at almost the precise spot where long ago Saboo had dug one-eyed Shambhu's grave, on the night we found the coins.

Lowering the pouch into the pit, she carefully shovelled

the mud back with her hands and a small piece of plywood which was lying nearby. She was full of nervous energy, like a little old monkey, and I was afraid she might stumble or slip into the pond. I waited until she had finished her task and slipped off hurriedly so that I was back in bed a good ten minutes before she returned.

Grandmother's increasing abstraction, her detachment, her inexplicable remoteness had affected me much more than I betrayed. Outwardly I was a happy and normal child, although I could already see from the looks on male eyes that things were changing and that my mother's fabled beauty and grandmother's legendary charm had begun their genetic renewal.

Thirteen is a confusing age for a girl; there is turmoil and agitation in the body and the mind and even the environment. When I began my menses, I knew nothing of what to expect. I though perhaps I had hurt myself without noticing and earnestly approached my grandmother for help. I showed her the dark blood spots on my bedclothes and on my frayed kameez. 'Should we call the doctor?' I asked, and was quite unprepared for the stinging slap my query provoked. Another slap, and I was consigned to our room, with orders not to emerge until instructed.

'Nothing but trouble,' grandmother gabbled, for her teeth had begun to foil her, 'this girl is good for nothing but trouble from now.' A look of pure virulent hatred crossed her face. She looked like a wicked old witch, and I hated her passionately and with all my heart.

Phoolwati stepped into the breach. When Phoolwati came to know of my condition, she brought me a collection of old rags and towels and instructed me in their usage and disposal. 'And don't forget, you are not to step into the temple compound,' she said firmly. 'You are impure for a few days and we can't offend the gods.'

I could not understand. 'It's not my fault,' I protested, 'I haven't done anything wrong. First grandmother gets upset and now you! Why, Phoolwati?'

Her reply surprised me. 'It's not like that in our part of the world, Gudiya,' she said in her melliflous Bihari voice. 'In our village we celebrate the arrival of womanhood, the descent of the Devi. But then your grandmother is an old lady; she has to manage the temple. Perhaps she doesn't want you to grow up; she would have preferred a little girl who would sit on her lap and listen to fairy tales forever.'

'I'm too old for fairy tales,' I said indignantly. 'I know all about life. And besides, according to all of you I am a woman now.'

She gave me a hug. 'Yes you are,' she said, 'you are a woman and we women need to stick together. Now that you are an adult, not a little girl, we can be friends.'

The next day, as I sat confined to the small room, exiled from the temple, denied a bath, cursing the womanhood that had so improvidently descended upon me, Phoolwati brought me a present. Or rather, many presents—a length of ribbon, a set of bindis, a small mirror, a kajal stick, even a bright, shiny lipstick. I was overcome with gratitude, although I didn't express it, and looked disdainfully at her offerings as nothing less than the homage legitimately due to my grandmother's granddaughter. In my heart of hearts, I was immensely moved and resolved that I would never ever forget Phoolwati's kindness.

Phoolwati bought grandmother a pair of second-hand dentures. They fitted badly and made grandmother sound even more incoherent, but she did not want to offend Phoolwati and suffered them valiantly. However, she would take them off when she sang her evening bhajans, and sans teeth, sans dentures her voice would rise pure and prayerful and indescribably, eternally young.

It was Phoolwati who introduced me to the magical world of films, Phoolwati who bought me my first-ever ice cream, Phoolwati who gave me a rudimentary outline of the facts of life. She assumed responsibility for grandmother and me, and her cheerful corpulence gave an edge of reality to our strange existence.

She loved cooking. The food she made was oily and spicy and extravagantly flavoured. I would burp contentedly after a meal with her, and she would beam at me in approval. 'That's how you are meant to enjoy a meal, Gudiya,' she would say, 'even your body is saying thank you.'

Phoolwati suffered intensely from 'gas'. She would contort her substantial figure to improbable postures to ease its passage, coax it out through burp or belch. But an eternal spring of 'vayu' seemed to reside in her innards, and her life became an increasing torrent of internal turmoil.

'Then why do you eat so much, you foolish woman?' grandmother would chide her.

'Arre, what do you saintly souls understand; bhoga is the most difficult part of yoga,' she would reply laughingly, reaching out for the 'gasgo' tablets she always kept handy.

These memories seem to portray Phoolwati as a sort of

comic, cartoonish character, but nothing can be more inaccurate or further from the truth. Phoolwati's dignity, intelligence, perseverance and goodwill gave a stability and bulwark to my young self. We shared the same fiercely independent spirit, but mine had floundered in the confusion of identity and norms. Whatever or whoever I had lost in mother and grandmother I regained in abundant measure in Phoolwati's love and warm embraces, and her flatulence and mammoth bosom bothered me not a bit.

ELEVEN

*· cultural reference —
author does not help
the non-Indian reader*

A year after Shambhu's unfortunate murder, Phoolwati performed a shraddha. At first she consulted grandmother on what was to be done, but Ammi's eclectic gleanings of Hindu culture had provided her with little or no knowledge of the mortuary rituals of the Aryan race. She shrugged it off by saying that these things were not important, life was only a passage. Shambhu was dead before he died and in a sense not dead even today as he lived on in Phoolwati's mind. Phoolwati astutely judged that she was fudging and sent for the services of a Brahmin priest, courtesy the offices of Sundar Pahalwan, who had by now become her ardent admirer.

The shraddha ceremony was held in the temple and passed without event or mishap. On Lila's insistence, Phoolwati had a feast prepared for fifty-one Brahmins, amongst whom were included grandmother and me.

The next day the Brahmin priest who had conducted the prayers turned up again. He wanted to meet grandmother. 'I can sense that she is an extraordinary woman with remarkable siddhis,' he told Lila and Phoolwati. 'If even the dust from her mind were to settle on an ordinary mortal like me, I would become a better and cleverer person.'

Kailash Shastry was a man with a felicity for words, and this charming speech so moved Phoolwati that she insisted that grandmother, whose reclusiveness now bordered on the paranoid, meet the pandit.

The Brahmin was a thin, meek looking man. His starched white dhoti spread out in an exquisite fan to reveal surprisingly muscular calves. He wore thick eyeglasses and an air of supplication. In spite of his deceptively insignificant looks, when he talked, the very air sat still and the crows came out of their rookeries to listen. Pandit Kailash Shastry equalled grandmother in charm. Very soon her defences were down, and that special smile, reserved at one time for her brother who had been to college and the Englishman who might have been my father, flowered once again in wintry warmth.

Although she rarely paid any attention to me now, I hovered around the periphery of those enchanted conversations. There was very little that they actually appeared to say to each other, yet a lot managed to get said. They spoke in riddles and conundrums, exchanging nods and smiles and cryptic phrases.

Phoolwati was jealous of this new influence. 'That pandit, he is merely looking out for himself,' she told me angrily. 'He thinks he can get something out of your grandmother! I know the type!' However, she was always perfectly charming to his face and never betrayed her anxieties about the commercial influence he might begin to exert upon my Ammi.

One afternoon, when Phoolwati was particularly vexed by an attack of flatulence and the non-arrival of a consignment of marigolds from Ajmer to the flower mandi, the pandit offered to read her fortune. The lure of the future was something her inquisitive nature could not resist and, amidst many protestations about her janampatri having been cast incorrectly at the time of her birth by an ill-meaning astrologer, she extended her soft hand to be read.

The expression on Pandit Kailash Shastry's face as he confronted the lines upon Phoolwati's palm was one of intense scientific concentration, almost identical to the expression I saw on the face of the man who ran the watch-repair kiosk in the slum-market that had mushroomed near the construction site.

After examining her outstretched hands for an interminable while, the pandit looked doubtfully at her, at me, at grandmother and scribbled some notations on the mud floor with a twig. Then, inexplicably, his expression brightened. 'Behenji, is it the past or the future you are interested in?' he asked earnestly.

'Arre, Panditji,' Phoolwati replied irritably, 'even if you tell me my past accurately, that is no guarantee that you know anything about my future. Every chaiwallah in a radius of five miles knows my past—don't bother about what's gone. What's to come is what matters and no dakshina or money for prayers until your predictions come true. Nobody can make a fool of Phoolwati!'

Pandit Kailash Shastry was not in the least flapped. 'Simha on the ascendant, you are naturally very garrulous,' he said mildly. 'Your father passed away from this world when you were born. Two brothers but,' shaking his head sadly, 'a similar fate! And then your husband—he too departs. This kundali is too strong to accommodate any men. No son either! After the age of thirty-eight perhaps this dasha passes, and then you will meet a man! Aha, ha—what a man, a giant! Together you will rise to the very pinnacles of power and prosperity.'

Phoolwati was listening intently.

'But I have a brother,' she said, 'and he is alive and well in District Madhubani.' Panditji looked at her intently. 'He is your brother,' he said slyly, 'but not absolutely so, he is your half-brother. You understand me? After your father died, your mother, I think, found some other occupation?'

Lila's face wore an expression of intent righteousness.

'The zamindar employed her in the haveli,' Phoolwati said matter-of-factly, 'but it's not the past I'm interested in. Every mai-ka-lal in Madhubani will tell you that! What about my future? My health, tell me about that?'

'Vayu—wind—there is an excess of wind in your system,' Panditji replied. 'Storm, mental tension and wind. From February next year everything will change. There is a man, a very strong man, with whom you will enjoy everything that is to be enjoyed. When that is so, you can give me any dakshina you deem fit. One dhoti and a pan leaf with supari will do. Remember the words of this poor Brahmin! My words do not leave my lips lightly. Each word is unpremeditated. It flies into my mouth like a parrot, from God knows where, and, when it flies out again, there is some power which wills that my word shall be and remain true.'

'What about our Mataji's hand?' Phoolwati said brightly. 'Tell me about her past; I have always wondered, but she is so secretive about it.'

'Great souls have no past,' Panditji said agitatedly,' 'no past and no future. It is all the same to them. It would be sacrilege for me to talk about her past. I can see it here before me, like a cinema-scope—her history—but she is a saint, an embodiment of shakti. You have much to learn, excuse me for saying so, if you can dare to ask me about her past. Om Ma Shakti.' He touched grandmother's feet reverently and departed, muttering and shaking his head as he left.

As Phoolwati had predicted, that was not the last we saw of panditji. He did indeed seem to have a long-term interest in the temple and made an all-out effort to woo the three of us, not without success.

TWELVE

In the meanwhile, my secular education continued in the betwixt and between environment of St. Jude's Academy for the Socially Handicapped. With the instinctive sense of snobbery all children possess, we were acutely aware that St. Jude's was merely a missionary school, not a convent. It was administered by an obscure trust controlled by the well-meaning parishioners of the Church of the Redemption, British Columbia. The principal was not a Catholic or a Jesuit but a Parsi lady who rejoiced in the name of Roxanne Lamba.

I had felt a strange affinity with Roxanne Ma'am from the very first moment I set eyes upon her, for her pale ivory skin approximated my own gold-white one. We both knew we were different shades of brown from those of grandmother, Phoolwati and the rowdy, unruly slum children who swarmed the school. I wasn't then aware of the whims and vagaries and inevitable consistencies of melanin content, of how the cool climes of Persia knew and recognized the pallor of Samarkand skin or the glow of the white sahib's legacy.

Roxanne was an able administrator, and our small school, with its three rooms, two tents and port-a-cabin administration block, was run with flair and acumen. We had blackboards and swings and a sandpit and three reasonably literate teachers who under the stewardship of Roxanne Lamba drilled us valiantly in all aspects of empirical knowledge. It was thus due to the noble impulses of the parishioners of the Church of the Redemption, British Columbia to do good to others that I was inculcated at an early age with the right English accent. Had I been consigned by grandmother to the nearest Hindi-medium school, as would have behoved the granddaughter of the temple Mai, instead of a missionary school run by memsahibs, the story unfolding in these pages would have been possibly quite different—unless, of course, one followed Pandit Kailash Shastry's view that everything in life proceeded only on the paths ordained by fate, desiny and kismet.

Schooldays passed without event, perhaps because I never attempted to compare or reconcile my two disparate lives. I revealed a natural aptitude for maths. This delighted Roxanne, who taught all the sciences.

In the beginning our school had no uniform, and we could amble in wearing whatever we pleased. Grandmother paid no attention to my clothes. I wore whatever was given to me without complaint.

The year after Shambhu died, a delegation of do-gooders from British Columbia came to visit us on a situation-study tour. They decided that we were to have a uniform, and thereafter I proudly wore a grey flannel skirt and a blue blazer to St. Jude's. Phoolwati took over the maintenance of my uniforms; indeed, she took over my maintenance altogether, and I never had a button or a braid out of place.

All these factors combined to make me one of fortune's favoured in the school hierarchy. Gudiya Rani, for that was the name under which Ammi had enrolled me, always had a place in the school roll of honour.

Everybody at St. Jude's predicted a bright future for me. Pandit Kailash Shastry concurred. I overheard him talking to my Ammi one afternoon. 'The lines on Gudiya's forehead,' he said, 'these lines are to be seen in one in a million faces. Mukkadar ki Sikandar—Gudiya's destiny awaits her. No, not only wealth, fortune, position, for these are ordinary things, but wisdom, knowledge, good name, fame—the real blessings of the Almighty.'

The astrologer's enthusiasm found no answering chord. Grandmother stared apathetically at him. I still could not understand or reconcile myself to the abrupt withdrawal of her affections. Even my academic success left her unmoved, and her indifference began to breed an insolent hostility in me.

Only Lila managed to retain communication with her. She was privy to Ammi's long silences and tended to her every need with dog-like devotion. On a pragmatic basis, Ammi trusted Phoolwati implicitly. All aspects of temple administration, including funds, had been entrusted to her. We were no longer poor, the few coins rattling in the thali which had been mother's had magnetized an immeasurable amount of wealth to our temple. Devotees and well-wishers vied with each other in piety and generosity. Marble flooring, marble benches, marble staircases—it was no longer a mere shrine but a thriving temple complex. Although the architectural plan was doubtless random, a bizarre intertwining of the individual tastes and quirks of our diverse devotees, it had a certain baroque charm.

The profile of our bhaktas had also changed. As the Janta Flats neared completion, the labourers moved on to the next construction site, selling their huts and jhuggies to land speculators when they left. Babus and clerks moved into the Janta Flats. Our temple was the only one available to service their diverse religious sentiments.

Recklessly, we added deity after deity to our pantheon: Brahma, Vishnu, Mahesh—we had the holy trinity, and many more besides. A corner for Murugan, a niche for Lord Dattatreya, a section for the Navagrahas—we had crammed them all into the temple premises.

'There are no temples to Brahma except in Pushkar,' Lila complained to Ammi. 'Brahma is not worshipped by Hindus—everybody knows that!'

'This is Kalyug, Lila,' grandmother replied, an expression of abiding patience on her face. ' Everything is forgiven in Kalyug.'

Pandit Kailash Shastry too reproved grandmother for this childish eclecticism. 'A temple must be built with the vastu shastra in mind,' he said firmly. 'There are scientific rules that have to be followed! This is like a doll's house, not a temple. You can't round up each and every deity in the pantheon! And besides, Lord Brahma is never worshipped anywhere in India, except perhaps Pushkar and a few other places. You must remove the image at once, or at least brick it off. These are serious matters, Mataji!'

Grandmother replied with her usual vague generalizations. She had by now perfected the art of presenting confusing abstractions as exalted philosophy and converted her lack of specific religious knowledge into a gnostic strength. 'It is all Lord Krishna's leela,' she said obscurely, her garbled speech adding a further veneer of wisdom to her words. 'Sab guddi-gudde ka khel hai!'

THIRTEEN

I had developed a figure. My breasts were like torpedoes, and I had long legs and a very small waist. My skin was like my mother's, very fair. I was not, thank goodness, blonde like her, although my hair had a bleached uncared for look until Phoolwati took me under her wing.

I was beginning to realize that I was beautiful and the thought exhilarated me. I wanted to enter the world of glamour and excitement, a world I did not know and which, quite unfoundedly, I associated with my absent mother. What was, after all, the sum total of her realized romances? After being jilted by a harmonium player, she had eloped with a beggar! Yet I wanted more than anything to be like her—to be outrageous and wicked—to escape from the stifling piety that enveloped my beloved grandmother. Ammi rarely smiled now; she never laughed; she constantly disapproved of me. She was nowhere remotely like the rational and lively woman who had brought me up.

I realize now, in hindsight, that the personal loss of her affections made me misunderstand her almost celestial quiescence. The detachment that she had developed and her preoccupation with some elusive inward journey only aggravated my need of her individual attention. I began to hate her with a desperate longing. I needed to provoke and anger her, and yet when I confronted her and met the calm sanity of that wrinkled face I withdrew even further into confusion and hurt.

I despised my name. I don't remember if I ever had any other, but 'Gudiya' was what my mother and grandmother had always called me. I didn't feel like a doll; I had never possessed a doll in the entirety of my childhood.

I was constantly trying out unusual and exotic names which I felt were better suited to the new personality I was only waiting, chrysalis-like, to assume. Samina was a particular favourite, or else Shabnam or even Sharmila. Gudiya was so gauche, so wooden, so utterly lacking in mystery.

I continued to oscillate between my two worlds. My existence veered between the St. Jude's Academy for the Socially Handicapped and the Mataji ka Mandir, as our temple was now commonly known. Mrs Roxanne Lamba had plans for an impressive career for me, involving competitive examinations, perhaps even the IAS. Or else, she hinted, I could become a schoolteacher and educationist like her.

Her ambitions left me unmoved. I did not associate success with studies. 'Shabnam' or 'Samina' would be a film star or even a famous courtesan. I was sure she would be rich, very rich. I had only the haziest idea about what educationists or IAS officers actually did. If they were dowdily dressed and wore spectacles like Roxanne Ma'am, I wanted to have no truck with them.

Life in the temple was daily gaining in commercial activity and momentum. The crowds of devotees, the smells of incense, the sounds of temple bells—all these shut out even the sibilant murmur of the peepul tree. Two important changes had taken place in the temple routine. The first was that Pandit Kailash Shastry had set up office in the temple premises and was available for consultation from ten to twelve every morning and from four to six every evening. Phoolwati had even managed to procure a loudspeaker, which nestled in the temple spire and was wired up so as to broadcast Ammi's evening bhajan. We could be heard in a radius of a few kilometres. Grandmother's liquid voice leading, and the disorchestrated response of our devotees, became a feature of the evening life in our locality.

Sometimes Ammi, feeling eccentric and inward, would refuse to sing. At first Phoolwati tried to cajole her, but then, exasperated by her stubborn refusals, she hit upon a novel plan. She took to taping grandmother's spontaneous bhajans, and when Ammi was in a recalcitrant and disobliging mood, Phoolwati would simply play the tape over the public address system.

That Easter our school had planned an excursion to Simla. Roxanne Lamba and two other teachers were taking those students willing to pay fifty rupees all-inclusive on a three-day trip to the hill station. I sought grandmother's permission through the good offices of my friend Phoolwati, and it was granted. The fifty rupees was duly paid up and a small overnight bag packed in readiness of the coming

Friday, when we were scheduled to leave.

One afternoon, Pandit Kailash Shastry overheard me excitedly discussing the school trip with Phoolwati.

'When and where are you going, Gudiya?' he asked, the expression in his eyes blank beneath the magnifying-glass spectacles. I told him and he took out his red cloth-bound almanac.

'Friday is Amavasya,' he said. 'It is a moonless night. Where did you say you were going?'

'Simla,' I repeated impatiently.

'Towards the north,' he murmured speculatively and undertook some rapid calculations. After a few moments of contemplation, he informed Phoolwati that I was not to go anywhere.

I could not believe my ears. Nobody except grandmother had ever told me what to do or not to do. I turned to Phoolwati in surprise.

'But why can't she go, Panditji?' Phoolwati asked. 'After all, there has to be some reason?'

Panditji looked grave. 'There are always reasons for everything,' he replied, 'but these reasons cannot always be told or explained.'

Phoolwati was concerned and worried. She sought grandmother's opinion on the matter. 'Let the girl go if she wants to,' grandmother opined. 'If one were to start listening to these astrologers, the second foot would never follow the first. I am ready to undertake any journey on an Amavasya night!'

But Phoolwati was not entirely convinced. She discussed the matter with panditji again, and then, without telling me, went to St. Jude's and withdrew my name from the holiday list. Mrs Lamba was reluctant to refund the fifty rupees, but somehow Phoolwati managed that as well.

I was bitterly disappointed. I wept and didn't eat my dinner, but Phoolwati didn't yield. I vowed never to speak to Pandit Kailash Shastry again.

Roxanne Ma'am was upset and became even more so when she came to know of the reason for my withdrawal. 'But this is superstition,' she murmured, 'blind, foolish superstition. It is charlatans like this who hold our society back. I insist that you join us, even if I have to pay the fifty rupees myself. Please inform that ignorant woman of my decision.'

It was, of course, the intractable will of 'that ignorant woman' that triumphed, and I did not go to Simla after all.

FOURTEEN

fetal position?

On Good Friday, the day I had been scheduled to leave for Simla, grandmother died. I found her lying in bed in an unnatural position. She was curled up in an umbilical pose, one hand a little raised as through warding off attack, an expression of entreaty on her face. A thin stream of dried-up spittle clung by the side of her chin.

I had never seen a dead person before, yet even without touching her or feeling her pulse I knew that she was indeed dead, that the unknown assailant was Lord Yama.

I could not understand what she was pleading for, why she had that beseeching look on her face. It made me pity her; it stirred up all the strangulated, suppressed love I bore her. My Ammi was all I had. I had been secure in her immortality.

I began weeping. I shed more tears than I had when mother left or when the Simla trip was cancelled. I lay prostrate by her cot and beat my head on the floor until I thought it would burst.

Lila came in to check why grandmother was not up till so late. When she saw Ammi's body on the bed she went stiff with shock and collapsed on the floor near the door right where she had been standing. It was left to me to run out and inform Phoolwati and the pandit.

They rushed to Ammi's room. Pandit Kailash Shastry hitched up his dhoti and raced there faster than I thought possible. Phoolwati slapped Lila tightly across her cheeks to revive her. They stood staring at grandmother's mortal remains. She looked small and pitiful, lying there on the cot. Phoolwati began weeping and the pandit settled himself crosslegged in a corner of the room and went into a trance.

Grandmother's death quickly became a real tamasha. When he returned from his meditation, Pandit Kailash Shastry sent me out of the room, insisting that my presence there was inappropriate. Phoolwati and I waited outside, looking around us at the suddenly unfamiliar temple.

Lila was not to be budged. Ultimately the Pandit had to relent and allow her to stay on. They were closeted inside with the corpse for almost an hour. When they re-emerged, grandmother was no longer lying on the cot. She was seated on the ground in an improbable posture, with one hand still raised as if warding off attack. I was too numbed to ask any questions, and in any case I knew very little of the rituals surrounding death. Perhaps all dead people were made to sit upright after death; perhaps it was a part of the decorum.

The public, who were by now thronging the temple precincts, were informed that my grandmother had not died, which was something mere mortals did. She had attained maha-samadhi, by voluntarily relinquishing her consciousness to the larger universe.

There was a stampede. The police had to be called in to

contain the mobs, who came, it seemed to me, not in curiosity but in genuine sorrow. Somewhere, somehow, my grandmother's incredible energy and power had touched and moved and changed them. They filed past the hastily executed cordons and barricades, to the courtyard where Ammi's body was propped up, surrounded by lamps and camphor and incense. Their eyes seemed to be asking some questions, begging some hope, from grandmother's lopsided figure and raised arm.

The arm, Pandit Kailash Shastry informed them (for it was he who was conducting the proceedings), was raised in blessing. Her samadhi was no ordinary samadhi, for even in death she remembered those she had left behind and gave them strength.

The mourners came with garlands and incense sticks as offerings, and soon the air was sticky and sweet and turgid with the smells of sweat and marigold and incense.

Pandit Kailash Shastry handled the crowds deftly. He gave the more persistent of them a flower or a leaf from the garlands which had been heaped upon Ammi. He was conscientious and efficient in the presence of death. I remembered how it was in this very capacity, as an undertaker, almost, that he had first entered our lives to officiate over the shraddha for Phoolwati's husband, one-eyed Shambhu.

The day passed in crowds and confusion and fasting. No food was to be cooked for the next thirteen days, and my stomach was already churning with hunger. In desperation I ate a banana which somebody had offered to Hanumanji and some mouldy sweetmeats I found in our room. Phoolwati got me tea from the tea shop, and in all the activity and excitement I quite forgot that my grandmother was dead and I was absolutely alone in the world.

Lila was still in a state of extreme shock. Phoolwati summoned her son and daughter-in-law and persuaded them to take her home for some rest. Lila left without protest, looking half-dead herself, her eyes blank and her face suddenly haggard.

Since grandmother had attained maha-samadhi, Pandit Kailash Shastry decided that she would be buried in the temple premises, seated in the lotus position, as was usual in such cases. Phoolwati advocated cremation, she wanted a funeral procession with a band and balloons and rejoicing, as befitted one who had lived to the age of ninety. Or so she estimated, for nobody was at all certain about Ammi's age, least of all me. No one consulted her next of kin about what was to be done and in any case I had no opinion on the matter.

My life had always possessed a haphazard and unreal quality, and now, when I contemplated my grandmother, contorted into an extraordinary death-pose by the indefatigable Pandit, my last link with reality snapped. This was not my Ammi; in fact, she had not been my Ammi for quite some time now. Yet whatever continuity and cohesion my life had ever contained had been gifted by her. What was to become of me?

On an impulse, I opened the old tin trunk which we had brought with us before Riyasuddin Rizvi decamped with my mother. The ghararas and cholis and chunnis and shot-silk bodices glittered and shone with a surreal light. I rummaged and searched until I found what I was looking for: an amber chunni sequinned with silver, embroidered with gold. It was associated in my deepest, most secret memories with the whinnying of a horse with kind eyes and the clatter of departure in a dense morning fog. I carried it out and draped it around my grandmother's fragile shoulders, hugging and kissing her as I did so. She almost toppled over, but Phoolwati and Pandit Kailash Shastry had gone to the tea shop for a snack, and there was no one to restrain me.

Meanwhile the crowds surged on, hungry for miracles. As none had occurred, Panditji expeditiously decided to announce one. The chunni, he explained, to a few close devotees, was a funerary gift from the Goddess Durga, Ma Shakti herself. It had mysteriously draped itself around the departed saint even as the mourners milled around her mortal remains. The chunni was saffron, the sacred colour—it was a sign, a blessing, a certain case of direct intervention from the cosmic powers.

The miracle created the expected stir. Even Pandit Kailash Shastry seemed convinced by his own interpretation of events. The crowds surged forward to witness the hand of God. They pushed and jostled for a sight' of that other-worldly chunni. The offerings of flowers and coconuts piled up and had to be continuously removed. They were taken back to Phoolwati's shop, from where she recycled them to the next batch of visitors.

On Pandit Kailash Shastry's instructions, Phoolwati and I undressed grandmother and bathed her with Ganga jal. After that we rubbed her body with ashes and sacred vibhuti. I averted my eyes from the sight of her nakedness, but

Phoolwati seemed not in the least embarrassed.

After this we wrapped her still-seated figure in two lengths of yellow cloth. Then the pandit came in and ceremoniously placed a rosary of rudraksha beads around her neck.

A sort of bamboo basket suspended from a bamboo pole had been made ready for the occasion. Grandmother was perched on this and carried out back into the courtyard, where a circular grave, about five feet deep, had been dug for her.

The sounds of castanets and temple bells and the tears and wails of her bhaktas echoed through the temple. Buckets of salt were poured into the pit, and then grandmother was lowered in, her legs still crossed in padmasana and her arm raised in benediction.

Lila had returned, accompanied by her son, to witness the blessed event. She was looking better now, the colour had returned to her face, and her movements had an unaccustomed energy. Suddenly she broke away from the crowd and rushed to the side of the pit. With a swift rapid movement she hurled her gold chain and bangles into the grave.

Her son looked on, horrified, not knowing how to react. The crowd watched curiously as Lila hesitated and then plunged into grandmother's grave. Phoolwati pushed her way forward through the surging crowds and tried to pull her out. Phoolwati's size and weight counted for nothing against the manic strength which Lila seemed invested with. She was quite unequal to the struggle and for a moment I thought she too would topple in after Lila, crushing my

Ammi with her enormous frame.

Pandit Kailash Shastry took over. Looking very fierce, he murmured something into Lila's ear. She considered what he had said for a while and then obediently clawed her way out. Her son led her away, looking quite rueful about the loss of the chain and bangles.

The ceremonies continued. Pandit Kailash Shastry filled up the hole with salt until it reached grandmother's neck, pressing it down until the head was immoveable.

Phoolwati put her arms around me and ushered me inside. The learned Brahmins picked up the coconuts from the pile in the basket that had been kept ready for the purpose and systematically set about smashing Ammi's skull. Inside our room, deep in Phoolwati's sweaty embraces, I could hear the muffled sounds of coconuts breaking, somewhere in the course of which the prana spilled out of grandmother's cephalus.

When we returned to the courtyard, the samadhi had been covered up again, and an oil-lamp was flickering on the spot where she had been buried, along with a heap of rice and flowers.

Pandit Kailash Shastry gave me a lit stick of incense and told me to place it by my grandmother's samadhi. The Brahmin priests were distributing the shards of coconut, and the crowd scrambled for the fragments, kissing them reverently as they received them.

Phoolwati appropriated a basketful of coconut shells to sell as relics. The tears were rolling down her cheeks. 'I have lost my guru, Gudiya,' she said forlornly. 'You are all that I have left.'

Grandmother's death and burial were reported in the *Evening News,* and a vernacular magazine sent a journalist and a photographer to cover the event. They did not talk to me, or even to Phoolwati, but only to Panditji, who described himself as her 'leading disciple'.

The night after she was buried, I moved in with Phoolwati. I took the old tin trunk, with its glittering memories, and my few meager possessions. The gold coin I had secreted away from grandmother's treasure lay safe in the depths of the trunk.

It was strange to sleep without grandmother, to be without the sounds and smells of the temple, away from the presence of the peepul tree. I tossed and turned all night, missing its comforting whisper as I knew my familiars missed me.

I could cease to be Gudiya now, perhaps I could even start to be Shabana or Samina or Sharmila. All that was known and familiar and sure had passed, and the future held in its palm every possibility and impossibility.

Contrast between the ending of the chapter and the start of another

FIFTEEN

Life without grandmother continued much as before. In death all activities in the temple simply began to revolve around her absence. Lila escaped from her son and daughter-in-law and set up vigil near grandmother's grave. She would not eat or drink or sleep or bathe. Having set up her asana on a decaying moth-eaten deerskin, she remained immobile for the entire period of formal mourning, not leaving her post, as far as I could make out, even to go to the toilet.

Everybody was extremely busy with all manner of mysterious and arcane ritual. There were lamps that had to be kept constantly alight, flowers to be offered and removed, lobhan to be burnt, prayers to be said, constellations to be propitiated. Above all, the crowds, the surging throngs of devotees, had to be handled with tact and patience.

This last task Pandit Kailash Shastry gratefully handed over to Phoolwati, whose administrative talents shone before the challenge. Each visitor to the temple was presented with a coloured picture postcard of Ammi, along with a piece of coconut and a small card which proclaimed: 'Blessings from the Motherhead'. There were orderly lines and neatly cordoned queues, and something about Phoolwati's substantial presence prevented the scores of distraught mourners disintegrating into a riot.

We were all so busy that we didn't have a moment to grieve. At the end of the day Phoolwati would fling herself into bed and beg me to press her calves. The pressure of my adolescent arms was insufficient to give her relief, and she would entreat me to tread over her legs with my bare feet, which I obligingly did.

I felt like a mountaineer, cautiously traversing up her enormous thighs and then back again, gently applying pressure on her knee caps, on to her calves, then giving her a little tickle on the soles of her feet before jumping off.

Phoolwati was unnaturally ticklish, and when I massaged the soles of her feet she would explode into paroxysms of uncontrollable mirth. Then we would both fall silent, shamed by our unseemly behaviour, and reflect afresh on grandmother's death.

All of us were a little unnerved by the almost fanatical fervour of Lila's grief. She had begun to treat her mourning as a vocation. She would sit by the samadhi, a rather silly smile stuck to her face, and mutter mysterious and unintelligible prayers to herself in a loud half-breath. Sometimes a tear would wander down her cheek, sometimes a sob would replace the smile. Phoolwati was of the conviction that she had gone mad, but Pandit Kailash Shastry, who had always been partial to Lila, opined that it was only an indication of a latent mysticism.

Lila's family made a few half-hearted attempts to woo her back, but after she had thrown her gold jewellery into my Ammi's grave, I could sense that they had somewhat lost interest in her.

The beggars had established themselves under the mango tree. Now that grandmother was gone and there was no fear of her ire, they felt free to visit her samadhi. They came punctiliously every day and filed past her grave in a most humble and befitting manner. Their piety met with a somewhat stony reception from the custodians of grandmother's legacy. Pandit Kailash Shastry, who had firmly advocated their right to squat under the mango tree, saying that there was always a place outside a temple for beggars, for were we not all beggars in the house of God, did we not all essentially arrive at a temple to beg, and so on, this same Pandit Kailash Shastry was now disconcerted and even angered by the temerity displayed by the three lepers in breaking the unspoken taboo and actually setting foot inside the sacred temple precincts.

Phoolwati's sense of decorum was equally outraged, and she scrupulously refrained from giving them, even her special friend Bhurroo, any of the packets of coconut with the 'Blessings from the Motherhead' card which she so liberally distributed to our other visitors.

Only Lila treated them with any kindness, sometimes even bestowing a gracious blessing on them when they filed past the samadhi.

The atmosphere in the temple was otherwise generally homely and cheerful. The pandit, who spent all of his day and even some of his nights at the temple, was to be glimpsed in the morning with a neem twig in his mouth, energetically cleaning his teeth. He had also of late developed a nervous habit of flapping his dhoti about, as though airing his privates. Both Phoolwati and I found this hilarious in the extreme. We would wink at each other, while maintaining a straight face, and only give vent to our hilarity when we were safe within the confines of Phoolwati's hut. Once alone we would abandon ourselves to laughter and take turns imitating him.

A sense of community and camaraderie prevailed. There were at that time no major tensions, and all of us felt virtuous and contented. The pandit performed the panchdana on grandmother's behalf. Gold, clothes, grain and cows were distributed in the course of a solemn ceremony to several not so needy looking Brahmins, rumoured by some malcontents to be Pandit Kailash Shastry's relatives. Since he could not make the ritual gift of land, having none to give, he endowed the Brahmins with a symbolic bowl of earth contained in an earthen pot.

The flow of visitors did not in any way abate, and the constant bustle and activity gave us a feeling of energy and momentum. Encouraged by the crowds, a temporary colony of beggars had mushroomed outside the temple. They seemed scarcely human. They were more like monkeys, plucking nits from each other's hair and scratching themselves indecorously, except when they sighted a prospective donor, in which case they expeditiously assumed a posture of extreme distress and desolation.

I was sure that grandmother's spirit, wherever it was suspended, would respond negatively to them, but Phoolwati assured me that it was all right, for wherever she might be, grandmother was bound to be beyond all this by now.

I was very comfortable, quartered with Phoolwati. I felt secure and safe and loved, and, with a little exercise of the positive imagination, I managed to somehow amend and correct my memories of Ammi, recasting her in the role of a beloved and benevolent grandmother.

SIXTEEN

Roxanne Lamba's house was quite close to the temple, but it was as far away from my world as anything could ever be. She invited me there some days after grandmother's death. A uniformed chauffeur sought me out at Phoolwati's hut with a note from Roxanne Madam, offering her condolences and inviting me for tea the next day.

I had stopped attending school after grandmother's death. Although I knew how Phoolwati felt about Roxanne Ma'am and the Simla trip fracas, I showed her the letter. She sniffed sarcastically and her huge bosom heaved in contempt, but she admitted that there could be no real harm in my going there.

Roxanne's house was simply enormous. It had 'Sharp House' emblazoned in gold on the wrought-iron gates, which an imposing looking chowkidar opened with a smart salute.

I knew that Roxanne Ma'am was well-off and that her family owned 'The Sharp Blade Company'—an old and respected firm of blade manufacturers and distributors. Still, her wealth startled me.

'example of division within society

I had not imagined that anybody could be so rich. The interiors glittered with chandeliers and lamps and carved mirrors. Everything smelt different—of flowers and heady unknown smells. It even felt different, soft and cushioned and textured. I simply could not understand why anybody who could live like this would wear dreary clothes and thick spectacles and busy themselves with the St. Jude's Academy for the Socially Handicapped.

Even Roxanne Madam looked different. She was draped in a diaphanous chiffon sari with a soft floral design and a low-cut blouse that showed her breasts. She was still wearing glasses, but this pair, which I came to think of as her 'home' pair, were shaped differently from her usual practical square frame. They were elongated and elegant and made her look like a cat-woman.

'I was so sorry to hear about your grandmother,' she said, 'it was such a shock. In a way I'm glad you didn't come to Simla after all—it would only have made it more difficult for you.'

Something, perhaps the way she said it, brought grandmother's death down to the realms of the everyday and the ordinary. I responded to her polite condolences by having another chocolate pastry. We were still not cooking any normal food and I was tired of the tea and bananas with which Phoolwati kept me going.

Two pastries later, I found that I was weeping. A torrent of hot tears was flowing down my cheeks. Roxanne Ma'am held me in a perfumed embrace and consoled me.

'Don't cry, child,' she said. 'Your grandmother is a fravashi now. Her spirit is watching over you. But her urvan, *improper use of English*

her soul, needs to be free. Don't hold her back, my darling.'

I couldn't understood what she was talking about, but no one had ever called me darling before. It made me feel better and I stopped crying. She gave me a fragrant handkerchief, and announced that the chauffeur was waiting and would drop me back whenever I was ready. As I got up to leave, she bent over to kiss me. Her lips brushed against my forehead and again I was assailed by that compounded olfactory essence of wealth and assurance.

The chauffeur dropped me back to the temple compound. As I got off I found another car parked before the main gate—a ramshackle old Ambassador which had seen better days. It was disgorging a convoy of sadhus and holy men—bearded, saffron-clad passengers with white ash smeared on their foreheads and fierce eyes. I looked at them apprehensively but they did not even notice me.

I walked into our room to find that everything had changed. I had been dislodged. My cot had been moved out, and so had grandmother's. There was a large dhurrie spread over the floor. A low dais had been set up at one end with white mattresses and bolsters. An enlarged colour portrait of grandmother, covered with garlands, hung on the wall. A photograph of Pandit Kailash Shastry graced the other wall.

I was bewildered. This was my room, my cot—whatever was the Pandit doing in my territory? Now he entered the room, followed by the swarm of sadhus I had seen at the door.

They settled themselves lugubriously on the dhurrie, murmuring a series of 'Hari Oms' and 'Jai Hos' as they adjusted their flowing saffron robes. I could make no sense of it and was about to leave the room when Pandit Kailash Shastry stopped me.

'Jai Mata ki! Gudiya, what brings you here? What a surprise,' he said, and steered me towards the photograph of my grandmother.

'This is the last legacy of our late revered Mataji,' he announced solemnly to the assembled gathering. This information was greeted by another buzz of 'Jai Hos' and 'Hari Oms'.

They stared at me incuriously, their glazed eyes still and unmoving, and I began to feel a strange chill of fear travelling down my spine. These were real holy men, the genuine article, not like my grandmother. Suppose they were to find out the truth about us? They had mystical powers—like Pandit Kailash Shastry, they knew everything. They knew about the glittering ghararas in the tin trunk and the gold coin I had stolen; they knew about my wicked mother. Perhaps they even knew where she was; perhaps they would summon her to come and take me away.

Fear turned to panic. Suddenly I could hear the sibilant murmur of the peepul tree, and there was Magoo swaying seductively on the lower branches, her face grinning in a terrible fixed way. I tried to will her away, but she refused to go. One-eyed Shambhu joined her, and then, out of the corner of my eye, I saw Riyasuddin Rizvi, entwined from the waist with my beautiful mother. They were grinning hideously.

Sweat beaded my brows, and the room began circling around me. I blacked out. When I awoke I was lying in Phoolwati's hut, in the large double bed which occupied most of the living space.

SEVENTEEN

The next day, Roxanne Madam's chauffeur was at our door again. Madam had summoned me home, he informed Phoolwati.

'Madam-Shadam be damned; my Gudiya is too ill to move,' she replied, and banged the door on his face.

A little later a flustered Roxanne had materialized in Phoolwati's hut and was fussing by my bedside. 'You poor child,' she murmured, 'I had no idea!' Before I knew what was happening, I found myself bundled into her long black car with Phoolwati in the front seat beside the chauffeur.

Once at Sharp House, I was half-carried, half-supported upstairs by Roxanne and Phoolwati. A more incongruous pair of women would be difficult to find, and I could not disloyally help but observe how fat and malodorous Phoolwati was. She was huffing and belching with the strain and her plump face had turned a mottled shade of purple.

Of course she was not too tired to examine Roxanne's home with unabashed curiosity. It was evident that she was immensely impressed by the opulence of our surroundings, and that her quick darting gaze was taking in every detail of the environment.

She clearly approved of the curve of the bannister and the bounce in the carpeting. When she encountered the one-armed Venus de Milo with the naked breasts at the turn of the marble staircase, her gaze turned rigid, but it softened again at the glitter of the green-glass chandelier and the two gilt cupids cavorting above the carved mirror at the first floor lobby. I sensed her open puzzlement at Roxanne's dull brown sari and horn spectacles and witnessed the quick mental revision of her earlier estimate of Roxanne's worth.

Finally, the two of them deposited me on a soft bed that all but swallowed me up. A forceful looking man with a shock of grey hair strode into the room. He had thick bristly eyebrows and hair grew out of his ears. A look of mild irritation rose on his face. 'Hello, who is this?' he asked, his quick eyes taking in Phoolwati's full figure and my inert one.

There was a stilted formality in Roxanne's voice as she introduced her husband. 'This is Gudiya,' she said, a little apologetically. Then, as an afterthought, 'And this is Gudiya's aunt, Phoolwati.'

She did not get the name right, she pronounced it 'Poolwati'. Nor could she keep the disdain out of her voice. I felt embarrassed. Phoolwati was not my aunt. She was not like my beautiful grandmother or my even more beautiful mother—she was one-eyed Shambhu's wife and she lived in a hut and had a problem with her 'gas'.

As though moved by telepathy, Phoolwati chose that very moment to ease out a long and martyred belch. Roxanne looked startled, even frightened, and her husband hastily left the room.

'I will keep Gudiya here till she gets better,' Roxanne informed 'Poolwati' in her broken Hindi. Phoolwati's fighting spirit had quite departed, and she readily acquiesced.

Dinner was sent up to my room in a tray. I ate with the ferocity of a starving animal. After I had finished every morsel of the chicken, I examined my new room. From the very beginning I assumed, without foundation really, that there was something permanent about the move and that I would continue to live in Roxanne's house the way we had continued to live on the stretch of road where Riyasuddin Rizvi had deposited us seven summers ago. I approved of the pastel colours and soft textures of my new surroundings and decided that I could live like this forever.

The following morning, a doctor was summoned to examine me. He had a hale manner and a fund of jokes. He diagnosed that there was nothing wrong with me that could not be set right with a few days rest. 'She has been in a state of shock. A little fun and food, rest and recreation, and the young lady will be right as rain!' he chuckled.

On the second day after my arrival, Phoolwati returned. Something in her encounter with Roxanne had clearly struck a deeply competitive chord. This was a completely revamped and re-upholstered Phoolwati. She wore an expensive silk sari, patterned in yellow and purple. A thick gold chain festooned her plump neck and a patent leather handbag was slung about her shoulders. A new found poise seemed to have accompanied these sartorial changes, and her already abundant confidence had transposed into a cool assurance. She even shook hands with Roxanne and her husband, Mr

Lamba, before they settled down to discuss my future.

Even Phoolwati couldn't manage to learn English in the span of two days and I had to act as an interpreter. I discovered that Roxanne's husband knew how to speak Hindi, but he chose to stay out of the discussion. Roxanne came straight to the point and so did Phoolwati. I had nobody in the world and Roxanne was willing to give me shelter and support until they reached 'a solution'.

Mr Lamba interrupted us at this stage. 'I want to make one thing absolutely clear,' he said in surprisingly fluent and idiomatic Hindi, 'this is to be an informal arrangement, and a temporary one. At no stage are my wife or I thinking of adopting the girl.'

Roxanne looked at him reproachfully. 'Yes, dear,' she said softly. 'I think Gudiya and Poolwati already know that.'

'And another thing,' Roxanne's husband continued meaningfully, 'there is to be no exchange of money in this transaction. I think it is only fair that "Poolwati" should be aware of that.' He put in an immeasurable degree of sarcasm into the mocking way he enunciated her name, cruelly mimicking Roxanne's drawling Parsi accent.

'Arre, sahib,' Phoolwati replied spiritedly, in her lilting Maithili accent. 'Don't worry about your money on our account. We may not be rich like you, but we do have our izzat. By the grace of God, our Gudiya is not short of money.' Extracting a wad of money from her new patent leather handbag, she counted it out note by note and handed it over the startled Mr Lamba. 'Let me know if you require any more,' she said, triumphantly snapping shut the shining brass clasp of her purse.

Later, alone in my bedroom, Phoolwati gave a satisfied belch and employed some colourful and abusive phrases to describe Mr Lamba. 'Your Roxanne Madam is all right, though,' she said grudgingly. 'I must admit that I was wrong about her. Your grandmother was really a saint in mortal form; see how she is looking after you even now. Wah, what luxury!'

She leaned back on the gilt and satin chair and gave vent to another appreciative belch, then straightened up hastily as Roxanne entered.

'I want to thank you, Poolwati,' Roxanne said gently. 'You are a good person.'

I tried to translate that for Phoolwati, but as usual she was too quick for me. 'You too very good woman, Madam,' she said in English, as she adjusted the pallav of her sari and made a magnificent exit.

EIGHTEEN

The next night Roxanne had a dinner party. Sounds of music and laughter percolated in from the window. I wondered if this was how it had been, so very long ago, in the haveli with a hundred-and-thirty rooms, in the time when we were rich.

I crept downstairs. The drawing room was ablaze with light and glitter; it overflowed with the smells of roses and expensive perfumes. Bejewelled women in splendid silks, roars of laughter, the tinkle of crystal—I breathed it all in from the corner of the stairs where I had positioned myself, wedged between the bannister and a piece of marble statuary.

Roxanne discovered me there. 'Gudiya, I would like you to meet Mummy, she is here from Bombay,' she said in her normal schoolteacher's voice, flashing an absent-minded smile at her guests as she led me out of my hiding place.

Roxanne's mother, Mrs Dubash, was an ancient lady, covered with flashing diamonds. She was sitting very upright on a marvellously carved chair which was almost a throne.

Her voice quivered when she spoke, but I could see that her sharp eyes missed nothing.

'What a charming child,' she said graciously. 'I do hope you manage to keep her out of trouble!' Her eyes bored into me as she spoke. They were old eyes, ringed with wrinkles and glazed over with yellow film, and yet they had a look of humour and cunning and alertness about them. Her eyelids were daubed with mauve eyeshadow, which clashed horribly with her bright red lipstick.

'Well, what is it, child?' she asked amusedly. 'What are you staring at? Never seen an old woman before?'

I smiled at her, enchanted. 'You look just like my Ammi,' I replied. 'I am sure you would have liked my grandmother if you had met her.' I noticed that the chair she sat upon had arms like engraved talons. Serpents encircled the elaborate mahogany legs.

'And where is this grandmother?' Mummy said, tapping her scarlet fingernails on an elegant cigarette-holder as she spoke. Although I had seen Magoo and the other labourer puffing at beedis and cheroots, I had never actually seen a woman smoking before. I was mesmerized.

'My grandmother's dead,' I replied foolishly, still staring at the cigarette.

'And so shall I be, soon,' she replied. 'Perhaps we shall meet in the afterworld. You're a good girl, go upstairs to bed now.' When I returned to my room I examined my surroundings with renewed delight. I inspected the curtains, the carpets, the fitted cupboards. I had never used a cupboard. Everyone I knew, Phoolwati, Lila and the rest, all hung their clothes on a rope or kept them folded in a trunk or under a mattress.

All of a sudden I remembered my tin trunk. I had almost forgotten the gold coin that lay hidden in the folds of my mother's sequinned gharara. I wondered if it was safe and if Phoolwati could be trusted with the custody of what was after all my most precious possession. Knowing Phoolwati, I concluded that she would rifle through my belongings at the very first opportunity. I would have to retrieve the gold coin, I decided sleepily.

I dreamt of grandmother that night. It was a vivid dream, which featured two groups of sultry belly dancers, who between them held a veil which concealed a precious object. After much laughter and music, the veil was moved to reveal my grandmother, seated in the lotus posture as she had been at the time of her internment, with the amber chunni draped about her white sari. She summoned me towards her and, cupping my chin affectionately in her gnarled hands, asked me how I was keeping.

'Arre, Gudiya,' she remonstrated, 'why haven't you combed your hair since I died? It's all tangled; you'll get nits if you are not careful. And why are you crying? You know your Ammi will never leave you . . .'

Her voice dropped to a dramatic stage whisper. 'And before I forget Gudiya—don't leave your gold lying around! Keep it close to you, always! Wear it next to your skin! And never, never marry a Juddin!'

I settled down comfortably on her lap and together we watched the belly dancers resume their dance. I realized that one of the dancers looked very familiar. Something about the way she moved and her smile reminded me very strongly of somebody I knew.

Then suddenly it struck me. That was my mother!

I tried to point her out to grandmother, but Ammi's body had stiffened, rigor mortis had set in. I cried out to my mother, tried to tell her about what had happened, but the dancers had all vanished.

I turned back to grandmother in panic. Her eyes were open again and she was busy readjusting the folds of the amber chunni. 'Don't be afraid, Gudiya,' she said impatiently. 'Haven't I told you a thousand times that I will never leave you alone? I'll always be there for you, you silly child.'

I noticed the peculiar carvings on the chair she sat upon. It had arms shaped like talons, and carved serpents encircled the ornate legs. As I was wondering about where I had seen the chair before, I woke up.

It was on my third day at Roxanne's that I encountered the dogs. As they ran up to me, snarling furiously, I recognized their eyes. They were canine eyes, brown and excited in pursuit, but they held a blank red glint which stopped me short on my tracks. My mouth went dry with panic, and a scream froze in my throat. I knew where I had met those eyes before. They belonged to my friends and familiars at the temple, the spirits nestled in the whispering branches of my peepul tree. Why had they left their green sanctuary to hound me here?

A dull film descended over my eyes and I blacked out. Within the darkness befogging my mind, I could sense the rustle of the peepul leaves as they slithered in the arms of the evening breeze. I heard a disembodied sigh and recognized the sad, polite lady with the apologetic smile. 'Don't worry Gudiya,' she whispered, 'we'll always look after you. Don't be afraid. Wake up.'

I opened my eyes and looked cautiously about me. There were three dogs, three sleek enormous Rottweilers, trained to attack. They were straining at their leashes and barking furiously. I was so terrified that I hadn't even noticed that they were chained and that I was quite safe.

Roxanne's husband came to my rescue. He had grey hair growing out of his nostrils. 'Julius, Brutus, be quiet,' he said, 'Tommy, down, sit.' And indeed they became quiet and settled down harmlessly around his feet. They were dogs again; the presences had fled.

Mr Lamba looked at me curiously. 'Are you afraid of dogs?' he asked, not unkindly. 'Don't be. They can smell out fear.'

'I'm not afraid of anything!' I replied. 'My grandmother was the Mai at the temple and nobody can ever harm me. Nobody and nothing.'

He examined me through narrowed eyes, as though I was some exotic breed of animal. 'Is that so?' he said amusedly. 'And what about your mother? Where is she? Is she also as unafraid as you are?'

I could feel my face flush; I was suffused with shame and fear. Could it be that he knew about my mother? Perhaps he even knew her! Covering my face with my hands, I stumbled away and ran back to the safety of my room.

That night I was ill again. I was also homesick. I was tired of the formal atmosphere, of the uncomfortable gilt chairs and the pale white carpet I had been cautioned not to stain. I hated the stiff unbending servants with their air of secret condescension, and I loathed the bland tasteless food. I wanted to return to my own world.

The family doctor was summoned once again. 'I have told you, Roxanne, there is nothing the matter with this young lady,' he said heartily. 'She just needs to have a lie-down and grab forty winks.' He nudged me jocularly and gave me a reassuring smile as he switched off the light.

Roxanne returned and switched on the light again. Her eyes gleamed behind their thick lenses. She was carrying an eagle feather in her hand, which she placed carefully under my pillow. 'Shikasteh, Shikasteh, Shaitan,' she murmured. 'Ahriman Ahriman gajasteh Karu Kerdar.'

I listened sleepily, ready to doze off. But Roxanne wanted to talk to me. 'There is something you are not telling me, Gudiya—you're worrying about something,' she said gently. 'Has somebody been unkind to you? I have not spent as much time with you as I wanted to, but we are short-staffed at school at the moment. Remember that you can tell me everything. Don't think you are alone because your grandmother is gone.'

I found her kindness somehow offensive. 'I don't want to stay here anymore,' I said rudely. 'I want to go back home.'

Roxanne's tone changed—in a second she became once again the formidable Mrs Lamba, Principal of the St. Jude's Academy for the Socially Handicapped. 'Perhaps it's time you returned to school,' she said firmly. 'Another week of rest and you can resume your studies.'

As they left the room I felt a strange and unfounded resentment. Roxanne was nothing if not kind and I was, after all, living in the very lap of luxury. Yet, I missed Phoolwati's warmth and the familiar smells and sounds of daily life. As I lay down on the cold clean sheets and looked around at my carpeted room with its pastel colours and soft lights, I had the sensation of being held captive by unknown forces in an utterly alien world. I reached out under the pillow for the eagle feather and, holding it to my cheek, fell into an exhausted, dreamless sleep.

↳ significant

NINETEEN

I returned to the temple without informing anyone. Roxanne was away at school, and I knew that Mr Lamba had left for office, leaving behind a mess of boiled eggs and toast on the dining table, which the bearer had not bothered to clear up. The servants were smoking beedis in the garage. The chowkidar had taken the dogs for a walk. I slipped out unnoticed and ran all the way back home.

Phoolwati was at Shambhu's old tea stall, scolding the young steert urchin she had hired to preside over the tea kettle which was perpetually on the boil on the earthen oven. She was not at all surprised to see me and proffered a cup of hot tea in greeting. 'And bring Gudiya some biscuits, double quick,' she hollered to her assistant. As the ragged twelve-year-old Raju set a plate of nankhatai before me, I was transported back to that day so many years ago when grandmother and I had had that momentous cup of tea in one-eyed Shambhu's tea stall.

Phoolwati was looking at me sympathetically. 'Missing your home?' she asked understandingly. 'Let's go and sit with Panditji at the temple for some time.'

The temple was just the same as it had always been and yet already it was different. Some new construction was under way. Steel girders and bags of cement were strewn around the courtyard. The atmosphere had changed. It was charged with a new authority and movement; there was a sense of stability and permanence, but some element of timelessness and quiet, of sanctuary, had disappeared from the place. The idols, with their familiar faces and blazing crowns and robes, looked, as ever, supremely relaxed and slightly bored, but the devotees—and there were fewer of them around than had been in grandmother's time—looked a little ill at ease as they were herded around by one of Pandit Kailash Shastry's new saffron-clad acolytes.

'I don't encourage them to dawdle,' Pandit Kailash Shastry explained, after greeting us with the utmost affection. 'This is not a bus stop or a railway station or a dharamshala that people should park themselves here whenever they have nothing to do! This is a place of worship, not an adda.'

Then he showed us the new steel boxes, with Godrej locks fitted on them, that he had installed strategically about the premises. They had 'Donation Box' and 'Dan-Patra' written on them neatly in red paint in English and Hindi, and then an encouraging 'Thank You' and 'Dhanyavad' painted below. 'I'm trying to get things organized,' he explained.

'Panditji, I would like you to çast Gudiya's horoscope for me,' Phoolwati told him.

'The time has not yet come,' he replied, 'and besides, there are practical difficulties. I do not know her time or place of birth, and I don't think she can tell us either, can you, Gudiya?'

I admitted that I had no idea when or where I was born. I did not even know who my father was, and neither, for a fact, did my mother or grandmother. Of course, I said nothing of this to Pandit Kailash Shastry.

'I want to know only one thing,' I said, assuming a pert gaiety. 'Will I marry a rich man? And when?'

Phoolwati gave me a quick hard pinch on my cheek. 'Wait till you grow up, Gudiya; the age of child marriages is past,' she said, only half-jokingly. 'Look at me! Learn from my example! I was just eleven when they married me to that Shambhu—and he was already twenty-two! He had both his eyes then; it was only later, when he fooled around with the Daroga's daughter, that he lost one eye.'

'But your Shambhu wasn't rich,' I replied laughingly. 'I want to marry a rich man! A handsome, fair, rich young man with a motor car and a chikna white skin and a big dog and a chowkidar to guard his kothi—with an upstairs and a downstairs and a spiral staircase . . .'

'You will get all these, and more,' Pandit Kailash Shastry assured me. 'That I have already told you, just from reading your forehead. But that is not all you will get. Fame, fortune, sons, property, prosperity—that is your grandmother's aashirwad. Your grandmother was my guru. With her blessings you will never want for anything!'

'This is all just talk, Panditji,' Phoolwati said tartly. 'Gudiya's grandmother blessed you too; she gave you this entire temple, twelve hundred square yards of land already constructed! Or one could even say that you just took it—and now our Gudiya, our Mataji's granddaughter, you could say her only living descendent, is homeless, penniless. How are you going to honour the memory of your guru? Even the shastras are quite specific about this. The guru's family has to be honoured as your own, or else . . .'

Pandit Kailash Sharma's expression had changed. He was on his guard; he looked stern. 'Gudiya is welcome to stay at the temple, and she knows it,' he replied. 'She is just like my daughter.'

'And who will hold people's tongues?' Phoolwati continued acerbically. 'My Gudiya is a beautiful young girl. And that rich man with a motor car and bungalow—where will she meet him? Rich young men are rarely religious, if you will excuse my saying so.'

She got up briskly and pulled me up with her as well. 'Achha, Panditji, Ram Ram! I trust you will never be wanting in the execution of your duty,' she concluded firmly, and steered me away even as Panditji grappled for a reply.

As we were leaving the temple, we bumped into Sundar Pahalwan, the dada of our locality. Sundar was swaggering about as usual, surrounded by a handful of goondas and hoodlums. He stopped in his tracks when he saw Phoolwati. A violent blush suffused his dark countenance and a dimple surfaced on his left cheek as his face creased into an ingratiating smile.

Phoolwati was looking at him archly and her enormous bosom was heaving a little more than usual. 'Lost your tongue?' she said sharply. 'Such a Dara Singh hulk of a man, but with the courage of a mouse! Why are you so scared of Phoolwati, man? Will she bite you? Will she eat you up? Arre bhai, Phoolwati is just a timid woman, and you are a hero-wrestler. Just say what you have to say. You want to discuss business with me, don't you? Then say so! Come to my house at seven this evening, and we can discuss whatever you want to!'

Sundar Pahalwan was now Phoolwati's partner in her various enterprises. I could not but admire the peremptory way she had dealt with him. 'Is there anybody you are afraid of, Phoolwati?' I asked, as we reached her hut.

'Afraid-shafraid nothing. Your grandmother used to call me an avataar of Durga. Even when that Shambhu used to get drunk and threaten to beat me up, two kicks on his bums would settle him and teach him some manners.'

I noticed a few changes in Phoolwati's hut. A small steel cupboard had appeared in a corner of the already crowded room and a portable television sat proudly on a shiny new laminated cabinet.

I was puzzled, for Phoolwati's jhuggi did not have any electricity. She was looking around proudly, waiting for my reaction.

'Where did you get it, Phoolwati, and how will it work?' I asked.

'That Sundar Pahalwan fixed it up for me,' she replied offhandedly, 'it's battery-powered.' She was squatting on the floor by the gas ring in the corner of the room which doubled as a kitchen. I noticed that she had red nailpolish on her stubby fingernails and on her plump toes. She kneaded the dough with deft, efficient movements and soon the delicious aroma of chapatties cooking on the griddle filled the room. It smelt wholesome and good. As I ate the hot rotis with some of Phoolwati's fiery homemade pickle, I felt healthy and sustained and fed as I had not been able to feel with the elaborate cuisine of the Lamba household.

I was barely through with my second roti when Roxanne's chauffeur, Bhimsingh, peeped in through the open door, cap in hand. His immaculate white uniform gleamed in the dark room. Phoolwati, still on her haunches by the stove, eyed him with stony suspicion.

'Roxanne Madam is really worried about you, Gudiya Baby,' he said politely, without any trace of condescension for the humble surroundings. 'She wants to know when you are returning home.'

'Arre, you langur in a white uniform, can't you see that this is the child's home?' Phoolwati asked indignantly. I could see that Bhimsingh was taken aback by her vehemence, but he did not respond in like manner.

'So what should I tell Roxanne Madam, Gudiya Baby?' he asked deferentially.

'Tell your madam to go to some orphanage and pick up some waif there,' Phoolwati continued, her face flushed with anger. 'Our Gudiya is not some pet dog or kitten for your madam to play with and amuse herself.'

Just then Sundar Pahalwan's burly figure loomed up behind Bhimsingh. 'What's this, what's this?' he asked roughly, eyeing Bhimsingh with the utmost suspicion.

'This monkey has come here to take our Gudiya away,' Phoolwati replied, her bosom all a flutter.

Sundar Pahalwan flexed his biceps threateningly, then twirled his moustache for effect. 'So you want to take our Gudiya away,' he asked menacingly, lifting up Bhimsingh by the collar as he spoke.

The chauffeur was a tall man, but Sundar was even taller, and Bhimsingh hung suspended in the air like a puppet.

I was suddenly reminded of that day, many years ago, when Sundar Pahalwan had confronted my grandmother and tried to extort his haftha. My Ammi had not stood his nonsense, she had never conceded his slum-lord status, and she had worsted him with nothing more than her wits. Something within me snapped. I knew with sudden clarity that I could no longer tolerate this tussle for ownership. Phoolwati, Roxanne, then the Pandit and now Sundar Pahalwan—I belonged to no one, just as my grandmother had never belonged to anyone.

'Put that man down,' I said to Sundar Pahalwan in a very quiet voice, summoning from the reserves of memory all that I remembered of my Ammi's authority and strength. But Sundar Pahalwan was too engrossed in demonstrating his own muscle and masculinity. He continued to dangle the chauffeur by his collar. Bhimsingh looked extremely alarmed and made muffled entreaties to be let down.

'Will you just put that man down?' I shouted, and lunged at Sundar with all my might. It was like hitting a brick wall. I could not even dent him, but he was so surprised by my attack that he let go of Bhimsingh.

Now it was time for Phoolwati to be angry. 'You joker, I called you here at seven, and instead you stroll in any time and beat up my guests? Just who do you think you are, Mr Wrestler?' she demanded furiously.

Sundar was completely taken aback. I do not think he had ever encountered such vociferous opposition in his entire life.

'Forgive me, yaar,' he said to Bhimsingh, 'it was a mistake.' Bhimsingh took a long breath and lit up a beedi. 'Make no mistake, I'm also the son of a Thakur,' he said. 'But I'm an employee of Sharp Blades. I would never get involved with scum like you, even if our Roxanne Madam doesn't know any better.'

Putting on his cap again, he stomped out of the room.

I looked at the half-eaten chapatti on my plate and wondered if Bhimsingh had already left and whether it was too late for me to follow.

Sundar Pahalwan stood patiently by the bed awaiting sentence. Phoolwati's painted fingernails were positioned on her heaving bosom, and there was a look of anticipation on her face. They did not even notice as I crept out of the hut.

TWENTY

When I walked out of Phoolwati's house, I had no idea where I would go. I simply set out, convinced that life would continue to provide new destinations, as it always had. I took any road that caught my fancy, crossed streets completely at random, never checking their names, never following any set direction. A sense of great freedom penetrated my being.

After I had trudged along for what seemed like a very long time, I came to the edge of a dusty park. It was hedged in on all sides with henna bushes and iron railings. There was, as far as I could make out, no way to get in, and yet I could see people strolling inside. I had been walking for over an hour and I was very tired. D.T.C. buses and autorickshaws wheezed past me. I had an overriding desire to go in and sit quietly beneath a tree, but I could not find the gate. Finally I settled down on the pavement, oblivious of the damage to the new clothes Roxanne had bought me.

Suddenly a white horse clambered up the pavement. I jumped aside in panic, only to trip over and fall into the rainwater ditch. Astride the horse, bareback, was a very handsome boy. He observed my predicament with an amused smile, then dismounted with easy grace. Holding the white horse by its halter, he walked over to where I lay and helped me out. I was covered in a mess of mud and dead leaves and I had lost my sandals.

He was so handsome that I could feel my insides quiver. He had a perfectly proportioned nose and a noble profile. He looked like a Rajput prince. He was shabbily dressed and his polished leather shoes had gaping holes through which I could see his torn socks and dirty feet. Who was he and why was he riding a white horse on the streets of Delhi?

And then he was gone. I sat down on the pavement again. Perhaps he would return. But of course he didn't. After a while I got tired of waiting.

As I trudged along, I began noticing the neighbourhood, the things around me, where I was. It was a dimly lit part of town, there were no streetlights, only flat oblongs and rectangles of light that fell on the narrow lanes from the steep and crowded houses around. There was a strange silence surrounding me, a silence compounded of fog and darkness and the sounds of television and radio floating around forlornly. It was a silence full of whispers, of hushed confabulations, of things left unsaid.

Suddenly the lights went off. It was a power cut, and the televisions and radios went off as well, making the silence even denser. A child's sharp scream broke through the silence and the darkness, and the candles and paraffin lamps came out in a practised routine. I looked around me uncertainly. I wasn't of course going anywhere, but this circumstance was compounded by the fact that I was by now hopelessly lost.

There was a row of shops behind me. I turned back to see if any of them had a signboard that might indicate where I was. The first of these shops was a meat shop, where a tall candle lit up the gaunt carcasses, the dismembered cuts of loin and thigh. There was something reassuring about this island of light, and I peered in.

There were two men sitting inside the shop. They were lost in an intense conversation. 'It is impossible to understand Kalki unless you understand the nature of the Kalyug!' one of them said impatiently. The shadow of the other man fluttered and moved like a giant moth in the dark interior of the meat shop. 'That is precisely what I am saying,' he replied. 'When the times degenerate, the gods degenerate. It is Kalki, the god of the Kalyug, who will come riding on a white horse and save us from ourselves!'

I listened transfixed. My heart beat louder than usual, it literally hammered against my chest, and I felt I was on the verge of a great revelation. Just then the lights came on, the glistening joints of meat were no longer in shadow, a small black-and-white television was relaying the news and the two men were striding out of the room as though they were in a great rush to be somewhere else. I hurried off, and soon I was on the main road again. A bus lurched to a stop before me. Still drifting, still floating in that inexplicable state of suspension, I boarded it.

I found a 'ladies only' seat. Even though it was the evening rush hour, the bus was not at all crowded. I saw the city of Delhi, dusty and desolate, sprawled before me like a dying animal. The muttered obscenities of the bus conductors, the commuter's apathy, the pall of diesel—

everything contributed to the marvellous sense of freedom I was experiencing ever since I walked out of Phoolwati's hut.

I had no money to pay for my ticket. When the conductor reached my seat, I made a show of having lost my purse. 'It was here in my hands just a minute ago,' I protested, 'some pickpocket must have walked off with it!'

'No problem, meri jaan,' the conductor said crudely, making a smooching sound with his lips. 'Aur kuch de dena!' and he lurched off to the front of the bus.

It was getting dark outside. I had absolutely no idea where I was. The streets were crowded with habitation and through the windows of the bus I could see lit windows, bits of sofas, corners of bookshelves, television screens, lampshades, people. Everyone and everything seemed contained, defined, in context. Only I was alienated and at large.

The bus staggered to a halt. The few remaining passengers got off. We were at the depot. The bus conductor gave me a meaningful wink. 'Where are you going, darling?' he leered. I hurried off the bus.

Outside all was dark, strange and lonely. The leaves rustled in the strong February breeze, and, although the day had been warm, the evening was distinctly chilly. I had no idea where I was, but it seemed to be a government colony, the kind of middle-class area where clerks and their families lived.

To avoid any unwelcome attention, I began walking very fast with a sense of purpose, as though I knew where I was going and was in a hurry to get there.

The complexion of the area changed and I found myself

on a street with a lot of office buildings. Groups of families—pavement dwellers—were herded around merry little fires of newspaper, packing cases and twigs. The delicious aroma of cooking arose from shining brass pots bubbling atop makeshift three-brick ovens. Old women were telling bedtime stories to their children.

I hurried on, gripped by the sudden fear that if I dallied I might encounter an old and decrepit beggar and his wife who was my mother.

I realized that I was being followed by a man on a cycle. He seemed drunk and was humming fragments of filmi songs, not unmusically. I began walking very fast and before I knew it I stumbled over an empty handcart and fell face forward on the pavement.

The man on the cycle had also stopped but he did not accost me or trouble me in any way. A loud hiccup escaped his lips and I could feel his silent presence on the road, observing me.

I was afraid to get up. As I was struggling to my feet, I heard a murmur of voices from around the nearest fire. A young woman of about twenty-five came forward to my aid.

'I hope you are not hurt,' she said in a pleasant, courteous voice and helped me up. The drunkard on the cycle had lost interest and taken off, but another cyclist had halted on the road and was staring at me intently.

As my saviour led me away to her stretch of pavement, the cyclist followed, pedalling slowly to keep pace. When we reached the street light, he got off his bicycle and approached us.

'Stop, stop. What are you doing here alone?' he asked

me. I turned around and saw that it was the electrician who had been one of our earliest devotees. I had not seen him at the temple for some time now.

'What are you doing here alone?' he asked me again. 'Are you lost? Does your grandmother know where you are?'

I shook my head. I was too troubled in too many ways for any explanations.

'If you know her, bhai saheb, why don't you see her safely home,' the young woman told him authoritatively, after looking him over and sizing him up.

I followed her instructions meekly and, shivering from the cold and the shock, settled myself sidesaddle on the rear seat of the bicycle.

The electrician, whose name I had forgotten, pedalled slowly and rhythmically. It was a good half-hour before he deposited me at the gates of the temple.

'Won't you come in?' I asked as I got off.

'No,' he replied, 'I have stopped believing in God.'

As I didn't know how to respond to that, we were both silent for a while.

'Why?' I asked finally, for want of anything better to say.

He considered the question carefully.

'My daughter died,' he said at last. 'She was run over by a car.' He fell silent again. 'It was a Mercedes,' he added somewhat inconsequentially. 'How is your grandmother?'

'She's died too,' I replied.

His face registered shock, then sorrow. 'She was a good woman,' he murmured. Then he mounted his bicycle and pedalled off steadily into the inky darkness.

TWENTY-ONE

It was good to return to the familiar warmth of Phoolwati's hut. It was evident from the transparent relief in her face that she had been extremely anxious about my disappearance. She enveloped me in an enormous, smelly hug. Struggling to escape from the folds of her midriff, I saw Sundar Pahalwan sitting on her bed, with a bottle of country liquor propped on a table before him. He was intently watching a Hindi film on the flickering black-and-white television set.

He turned around to look at me. 'Oh, so you're back,' he said flatly. 'My men are out on the job searching for you.'

I maintained a sullen silence. There was no need to account for my actions to Sundar Pahalwan. Phoolwati sensed my mood.

'Lets go to the temple, Pahalwanji,' she said piously. 'Arre, touba touba, but you are smelling of liquor! Let's meet tomorrow—' a complicit wink to me, 'until then, Ram Ram!' She packed him off with a coquettish smile, and soon we were both comfortably ensconced in the enormous double bed, snug against the February chill under a brightly patterned cotton quilt.

'This Sundar Pahalwan is becoming a real nuisance,' she said complacently. 'All the time, it's Phoolwati this, Phoolwati that. I don't know why he is always pestering me.'

She looked at me meaningfully, but I remained perversely silent. 'I don't know what he sees in me,' she continued, twirling her thick plait around her fingers as she spoke. She looked absurd but quite charming, and I hugged her affectionately.

'You madcap!' she said indulgently, and continued her monologue about Sundar Pahalwan.

The evening continued in a merry mood. Phoolwati extracted a bottle of cough syrup from behind the window and persuaded me to have some as an aperitif before dinner. She glugged it down in copious quantities and when we were through with the bottle we ate some delicious potatoes and rice which she had kept readied for me.

She fell asleep without doing the dishes. My stint with Roxanne had left me more disinclined then ever towards domestic chores and before long I too had fallen into a deep dreamless slumber.

I awoke with a start in the middle of the night. This was not my room in the temple nor the soft pastel fantasy I had inhabited at Sharp House. In the distance I could hear the familiar rustle of the peepul tree. I was completely disoriented.

I remembered the tin trunk and my resolve to check its contents. Phoolwati was spread all over the bed, snoring loudly. I was pinioned under one of her plump arms. Extracting myself carefully, I crept to the corner where I knew she had deposited my trunk. There was no electricity, but the street light was sufficient to move by.

The key to the trunk dangled from a black thread Pandit Kailash Shastry had given me to wear, along with a silver charm. The old tin trunk squeaked and rattled in the opening, but Phoolwati was blessedly oblivious to the sound.

I rummaged around blindly in the dark until my hands encountered the hard cold feel of the coin. I hesitated and then took it out. Silently secreting it in the folds of my brassiere, I re-locked the trunk and crept back to bed.

I had a languorous dream in which I once again encountered the handsome boy with the princely profile. We danced around trees in the time-honoured filmi way. His eyes blazed with manic intensity, and my stomach was aquiver with a peculiar sensation, not in the least unpleasant.

When I woke up, I resolved never to return to Roxanne. The sounds and smells of Phoolwati's hut made it home as Sharp House could never be. There was something remote and unreal, a lack of energy and vitality in the way the other half lived. I had decided the sanitized life was not for me.

The question of my future never bothered me. Ever since we left the haveli, I had unquestioningly accepted whatever cards life had dealt me. Of course, there had always been grandmother to mind the details but in that sense I felt she was there still, watching, abstracted yet vigilant, from some not-too-distant heaven.

I was perfectly happy to live with Phoolwati. St. Jude's and the temple constituted the parameters of my life. Temple life was never dull. Furthermore, a sort of near-perfect understanding prevailed between all of us. The life of the community has a certain soothing impersonality, a sense of joint if undefined purpose. It was this which alienated me from 'normal' family life and made me unable to offer myself for adoption to Roxanne and her world. Even Sundar Pahalwan, with his odd and ever-increasing admiration for Phoolwati, had a surer place in my understanding and affections than Roxanne with her excess of charity and piety.

The evening bhajans at the temple continued as before. The audio cassettes that Phoolwati had so astutely taped were invaluable in keeping our regular congregation from falling. However, sometimes the tape recorder would pack up or the electricity fail or the batteries weaken. In time the tapes themselves began to spill out of the spools in a helpless mess, and grandmother's golden voice was all but set to escape to the other world. *symbolic that ultimately grandma will be forgotten*

Of course Phoolwati had assiduously maintained a back-up of the tapes, but she was adamant about parting with these. We were faced with the dilemma of how to structure the evening bhajans. In the meanwhile, Bhurroo the leper, Phoolwati's friend, was establishing quite a following under the mango tree. His stubby fingers became magically dexterous when they encountered the rough bamboo of his flute. Phoolwati's business instincts sensed an impending clash of interest, and she fell into an absolute panic about what to do.

Pandit Kailash Shastry was of the opinion that a short discourse by him on the values immanent in the Bhagavad Gita or something like that would be sufficient to retain the interest of our devotees. Phoolwati emphatically vetoed the idea; indeed she was of the opinion that such an option could only further alienate the slowly dwindling numbers of our regulars.

'Forget your philosophy-wilosophy,' she said, 'only Lata Mangeshkar could replace our Mataji.' She fell silent, her brow knit in concentration, and then, her face brightening, announced to a startled Panditji that henceforth she, Phoolwati, would lead the bhajans.

'But you can't sing!' Lila interjected. Lila had scarcely spoken since grandmother died. Indeed we had become so accustomed to her silences that we were all startled to hear her voice at all.

'I have an idea,' Phoolwati replied smugly, and there was something so unyielding in her calm confidence that we fell in line with her certainty and asked no further questions.

The next day a harmonium and a tabla were carted into Phoolwati's hut, followed by a music master and a tabalchi. The very sight of the music master and the percussionist threw me into a state of panic. I was reminded of my mother and was convinced that it was only a matter of time before Phoolwati too would depart as she had done.

Phoolwati, the tenderest of souls, sensed my despair and took pains to reassure me. She persuaded me to join them during her lessons, but the music master confirmed that I was not in the least musical.

'It will take a miracle to teach that one to sing,' he said, chewing complacently on a blood-red paan leaf as he spoke.

Pandit Kailash Shastry was requested to hold his discourses in lieu of the evening bhajans until such time as Phoolwati's musical education bore fruit. He was only too pleased to oblige, and soon his stern voice began to blast the evenings, amplified by the crackling mike, scaring away the crows, not to speak of the devotees.

A few morose old men seemed to like his style, but by and large it was not popular. Panditji's discourses were depressing, not elevating as Ammi's singing had been. When he was not foretelling the future, he was a charmless and monotonous speaker.

Phoolwati suggested that the pandit spice things up by introducing some astrological forecasts, but he protested, saying that such an arcane and intuitive activity could only be conducted in some degree of privacy.

'What about the newspapers?' Phoolwati persisted. 'They tell the future to everyone without making a fuss, don't they?'

He replied angrily that it was not the same thing at all and continued delivering his grim monologues on virtue and truth and dharma, while we waited for Phoolwati's musical talents to manifest themselves.

Her lilting Bhojpuri voice had always been musical. It was also very loud, which meant that the cantankerous mike would not present a problem. But there was something wrong somewhere. In spite of the music master's diligent demonstration of the scales and Phoolwati's persistent attempts to emulate him, it just did not sound right. 'Sa re ga ma,' she would go, stubbornly, again and again, determined to get there somehow, 'Sa re ga ma pa dha ni sa!' The music master would look at her despairingly, the tabalchi would smirk, and I would feel vastly relieved, safe in the knowledge that she would never elope with the percussionist.

In the meanwhile, Pandit Kailash Shastry carried on in

full steam. 'This is the age of iron,' he would exclaim, 'this Kalyug, where man and the world are all diminished!' The children in the audience would be fidgeting and the women gossiping in gentle whispers. 'Good and bad, godhead and human, all have got mixed up. That is the nature of the present. That is Kalyug! We all just have to manage somehow!'

Manage we did. The music master announced that he had done his best; he could do no more. Phoolwati made her debut. From the moment she picked up the mike, she was a star. Her infectious smile, her energy, her optimism, her spontaneity, all communicated themselves to her audience. The off-scale notes did not seem to matter. It was a miracle of sorts.

That was not all. Phoolwati had another ace up her sleeve. The next day her bhajans were radically different. She simply picked up a popular film tune and adapted the lyrics to religious sentiment. For example, 'Mera naam, chin chin choo' became 'Mera naam, main Shivji hoon'. Her bemused audience quickly got hooked and was soon roaring and hooting its approval.

Later, the Pandit said such songs were most unbecoming in a temple, but even he had to admit that they went down better than his discourses. 'It is Kalyug,' he said, 'after all, in this democratic age, what else can we Brahmins do but let the people have their way?' And he sighed philosophically, eyeing the day's takings.

TWENTY-TWO

In the meanwhile, school was proving to be a disaster. Having joined late, I was older and taller than most of the students in my class. St. Jude's had only up to the eighth grade, and I was already in the seventh. It was unlikely that I would be able to get admission to any good English-medium school. My stay at Roxanne's house had only reinforced my ingrained feelings of superiority, and I had become, I suspect, utterly obnoxious to both my teachers and my fellow students.

Although I was no longer so conspicuously Roxanne's favourite, nobody had forgotten our special relationship. This, combined with my status as Ammi's granddaughter, labelled me as being different from the other girls in my class.

We had a new teacher in school, a petite young woman called Malvika Mehta. She had graduated from the Delhi School of Social Work and ran a counselling programme for underprivileged students, where she advised them on what to do with their lives. It was taken for granted that none of us would continue with our studies; the boys were expected to become mechanics or television repairmen, the girls to learn sewing or take up employment in a factory or a creche until they were ready for marriage.

One afternoon, I was summoned to Malvika Mehta's room along with a group of other girls for a counselling session. She was extremely good looking. She had creamy white skin, jet-black hair, cut in a short, extremely fashionable style, and a lascivious mole poised over her succulent lips. She was dressed in simple clothes that I suspected of being very expensive. Something about her looks, her clothes and her air of total control aroused my instant and unprovoked hostility. She represented everything I most wanted to be and almost, but not quite, was.

Malvika Mehta examined the four of us. The other three girls in my group all came from disadvantaged but stable backgrounds. Anita was the daughter of a vegetable seller. Her father was an alcoholic, but he provided adequately for their large family. Madhu had a hazy past—she lived with a woman she claimed was her aunt; she was well-dressed and amenable and quite at peace with the world and her environment. Shivlata's mother washed and swabbed at several well-to-do houses; the father, who was a railway employee, had abandoned Shivlata and her sisters and was living with his second wife by whom he had two sons.

They were all clever and capable young girls and their stories were not dissimilar to mine. Yet they were not me and I was not them. Our ambitions divided us. They knew who they were, and they grasped, or glimpsed, what they had to become. My Ammi had taught me that anything was possible to one who aspired—my mother's life was a cautionary

[margin note: • fracture between dream & reality]

addendum to her exhortations.

Miss Mehta was quite insensitive realize differentiations. To her we were all birds of a feather. As students of the St. Jude's Academy for the Socially Handicapped, we were the hapless recipients of the combined goodwill of the Church of the Redemption and Miss Malvika Mehta personally.

She surveyed us aloofly. 'This class has been instituted to help you realize the untapped potential within . . . ' she said, tapping on the table with her ballpoint. An implacable resentment welled up within me at the sight of her glossy well-kept hair and manicured fingernails.

'All of you girls can achieve as much as your brothers, perhaps even more. There is no end to the world of possibilities if backed by hard work. Now I would like you to tell me, one by one, what you would like to achieve and why. Then we can have a group discussion on the subject.' It sounded rehearsed and insincere, but I was alone in thinking so.

The other girls responded eagerly. 'I want to be a school teacher,' Madhu said brightly, 'and help other children get educated and get good jobs.'

'I want to learn how to stitch and start a tailoring shop,' Anita replied.

'And I want to get married, Miss, and have lots and lots of children,' Shivlata said dreamily.

Those cool eyes turned speculatively towards me. 'And what about you, er . . . Gudiya?' she enquired, wrinkling up her nose distastefully as though there was something undesirable about the very name.

I was so upset and angry that I could not reply. Little

bubbles of spit formed around my lips as I struggled to keep my silence, for I knew that if I so much as opened my mouth I was lost.

'So, Miss Gudiya Rani, what is it you want to become?' she said again. She handled my name as if it were a dirty dishcloth. 'I don't know,' I replied, still maintaining control.

'You can't be a Gudiya all your life, you know,' she said amusedly, examining her long pink fingernails as she spoke.

Something gave inside me. 'Firstly, my name is not Gudiya, but Samina,' I retorted. 'And secondly, what I want to become, I don't need your help for.'

She raised her left eyebrow.

'I am going to become a . . .' I paused, as my mind scanned the pinnacles of becoming. 'I am going to become a film star and marry the prime minister's son,' I exclaimed wildly.

She looked bemused. 'Oh really,' she said weakly, 'that's very nice.' Madhu snickered, and Anita and Shivlata joined in the laughter.

The jargon of the temple spilled over into daily life. 'I curse you,' I screamed wildly, 'to become a she-rat in your next life!'

'And that's not all,' I continued, carried forward now by some afflatus. 'I will be the richest woman in the world, travel by aeroplane—and lock you up in jail, you witch!'

Miss Mehta led me straight to Roxanne Madam's office, where there was much contention and analysis about what it was that I had actually said. She insisted that I had used abusive language and called her a stupid bitch. I was equally vehement in admitting merely to the injudicious use of the word 'witch'.

The other girls were summoned. Madhu and Anita were neutral; they hadn't heard anything. But Shivlata testified eagerly to having heard me 'swear in English' at Miss.

The reproach in Roxanne Madam's eyes bothered me not a bit. I wanted to battle it out with my adversary, to prove that I was as good as her in every way, if not better. Still, some part of my Ammi's tact and good sense came to my rescue, and I rendered a very convincing apology. Roxanne was mollified, Malvika Mehta appeased, while I swore secret and terrible revenge.

I resolved to change my name, my identity, my very self. I became a creature of possibilities, unfettered by a past, totally involved in the process of becoming. All I lacked was a name.

I experimented with several. Gudiya Lamba—that was improbable; Sharp House and its sahib-log had offered me but temporary and undefined shelter. Besides, it was the Gudiya that was most offensive; it grated on the ears; it was everything I was not. I decided to rename myself 'Pooja', in honour of my favourite film star. All that remained was to find a surname.

I had absolutely no idea who my father was. This gave full scope to my imagination, and I became totally consumed by a set of intense and overlapping daydreams, where I was, variously, the daughter of an English Lord, an Arab Sheikh and a passionate blue-blooded bandit who was shot dead after secretly marrying my mother.

'Pooja Smith' (it was the only English surname I knew) didn't sound right. I flirted with 'Pooja Sheikh' for a while but finally settled on a tragic feudal past. I decided to become Pooja Abhimanyu Singh and to forever cherish the terrible tale of my parent's star-crossed love.

I practised a series of elaborate signatures, replete with flourishes. I carefully hoarded clues and signs of my new identity—pop music, dangling earrings, a regal look, a photograph of my father and a disposition towards revenge.

The photograph was purloined from an album I found in a junk shop. The kabadhi was a friend of Phoolwati's, and we had gone together to search for a second-hand dressing table for her room. I chanced upon a discarded photograph of a noble looking man with a waxed moustache. I liked the look of him and decided that he was to be my father.

Phoolwati was sceptical about my new identity. 'I understand your changing into Pooja, Gudiya,' she said, 'but Pooja Singh! Pooja Abhimanyu Singh! That's not even a Brahmin name! It's scandalous!'

TWENTY-THREE

A few days after the incident with Miss Malvika Mehta, Roxanne Ma'am called me home for a 'little chat'. Over a cup of aromatic black coffee and slightly soggy biscuits, she told me confidingly that she knew it was 'that woman's' influence which was making me so wayward and capricious.

'Come back to Sharp House and live with us again, Gudiya,' she said earnestly. 'You have a spark. You have potential. Education is a drawing out, not a putting in. I want to draw out the best in you.'

I drew back, repulsed by something in her tone. I had discovered a fact which, for some reason, shocked and disconcerted me. I was not the first or only recipient of Roxanne's unusual charity. There had been another young girl who, like me, had been brought to live in Sharp House, some five or six years ago. Nobody was very sure about what had happened to her. Rumour held that she had died, that she had jumped off the water tank atop Sharp House. The story was discussed in hushed whispers in school; it was everybody's favorite bogey story, and some girls even claimed that an inquisitive teacher had been fired from her job for asking Roxanne if the story was true.

I realized that despite, or perhaps because of, her extreme kindness, Roxanne Ma'am was not universally popular. She was a constant and favourite subject of discussion at St. Jude's. The girls and teachers all discussed her obsessively. They gossiped about her husband, who was supposed to be a 'real flirt'. They 'knew' that Mr Lamba had married her for money. They speculated endlessly about her fortune, which was still controlled by her mother. Sharp House exerted a powerful sway over the collective romantic imagination of St. Jude's. I was constantly pestered for salacious details of what went on 'inside the house', and when I refused to be drawn into such backstairs gossip I was dubbed a teacher's pet.

Something in this latest encounter with Roxanne's well-meaning insensitivity drew out a latent anger in me. Even Malvika Mehta's effrontery was more bearable—at least it could be tackled head on. The condescension implicit in Roxanne Madam's charity embarrassed and enraged me beyond endurance. Grandmother had inculcated in me a fierce sense of my own worth. I resolved that someday, somehow, somewhere, I would get even with all of them.

When I got home I was still scowling. Sundar Pahalwan was seated on Phoolwati's vast double bed, contemplating an empty bottle of country liquor.

'What's with you? Swallowed a toad?' he asked. I looked around the tiny room. Phoolwati was not at home, and, even if she had been, there was no likelihood of any privacy. I decided to go for a walk and stomped out, ignoring Sundar's well-meaning offer to 'liquidate' whoever was troubling me.

Four new shoe-box shaped concrete shops had come up a little down the road. As I passed them, a strange sight greeted me. A magnificently attired band, all gold and scarlet and braid, was perched full strength atop the flat rooftops. As I squinted up to look, an incredibly handsome face with intense eyes and chiselled features met my gaze. He was playing the trombone. He moved the heavy instrument away from his lips to bestow an inhumanly charming smile on me. It was the boy on the horse who had all but trampled over me outside the park.

As the band played on, our eyes locked in an intimate, encompassing stare. I stood transfixed, dazzled by his beauty. The music stopped and the other bandwallahs started shuffling down the precarious open staircase that led to the back of the shop. The 'Shiv Mohan Band' (founded 1968) had only recently taken up residence down the road. The white horse which they rented out for wedding processions was proudly tethered to the neem tree outside the shop. *quality of fairytales*

The boy walked down the staircase with the effortless ease of a prince. He leapt astride the horse and smiled at me. 'Coming for a ride?' he asked. There was of course no question of my refusing. He gave me a hand and I was hoisted up beside him, viewing the world from a different vantage point altogether. I was at about the elevation of a bus window but the sensation was very different.

We set off, weaving our way about the traffic. The horse's hooves clattered busily on the pot-holed Delhi streets. Our steed was not at all nervous of traffic and we raced busily through the mad afternoon rush, exhilarated, impatient, not quite of this world. We were galaxies removed from the timid scooterists with fat, sweaty women riding pillion and the hapless crowds of confused milling pedestrians so far below us.

It was towards the end of the monsoons and all the cattle from the neighbouring states of Haryana and Rajasthan seemed to have arrived to feast on Delhi's abundant foliage. Every now and then we would encounter a group of obstinate cows and the boy would rein the horse in and make a curious clacking sound.

I did not know my companion's name, but I was not in the least curious. Everywhere people turned around to stare at us. Young men on the tops of double-decker buses whistled and made lewd comments. At one stage, a crowd of street urchins gathered around us, shouting 'autograph, autograph', thinking doubtless that it was a film shooting.

At last we raced to a stop at a dirty municipal market I did not recognize. The boy swung gracefully off the horse and tethered it to an iron railing, leaving me, to my horror and mortification, stranded atop the beast. I was speechless with terror. Sensing my fear, the horse whinnied and raised its forelegs. I thought I would faint and fall off, but a small child came along, selling chana jor garam, and began stroking its nose. The horse relaxed, and so at last did I. I began looking out for my prince.

He was waiting impatiently outside the lottery stalls, where a group of disconsolate stragglers were going through the list of the day's winners with various grieving emotions. The lottery stalls, on makeshift wooden pushcarts, were huddled beside an open sewer which had been thoughtfully covered up with wooden planks to accommodate the rush of customers. The boy checked the winning numbers and then his tickets. An ugly scowl contorted his handsome features. Wordlessly he clambered back on the horse, and we returned to the river of traffic and diesel fumes.

He didn't ask me where I wanted to go; in fact, he didn't ask me anything but merely deposited me silently outside the temple gates. I had not realized that he knew where I lived, and I wondered what else he knew about me.

As for me, I was no nearer discovering his name. I felt too shy to question him outright. 'What's his name?' I asked, stroking the horse's glistening white mane, the thin fine strands of which looked like the hair of a very old woman.

'It's not a he!' the boy replied scornfully. 'Don't you know, she's meant for the bridegroom, and the groom only rides a mare!'

Before I could ask him anything else he had vanished in a cloud of dust. I realized that Pandit Kailash Shastry was standing behind me, staring reflectively at the figure with red braid epaulettes, astride a white horse, as it was eclipsed from view by a Redline bus.

'Who's that?' he asked pensively, wearing the expression of thoughtful scrutiny I knew so well.

'I don't know,' I replied truthfully.

'Well, I do,' he said. 'That is Kalki, the scourge of the Kalyug.'

That evening Phoolwati was indisposed and requested Pandit Kailash Shastry to stand in for her during the evening bhajan. I was sitting under the peepul tree, idly braiding and unbraiding my hair, when his rather flat voice crackled through the public address system.

'First there was the Satyug,' he intoned, in a particularly tedious way. 'That lasted 17,28,000 years. And then there came the Tretayug which lasted 12,96,000 years. The third epoch called the Dvaparayug lasted about 8,64,000 years. We are living now in the Kalyug, the age of misery and deceit. This Kalyug, our ancient seers have predicted, will last 4,32,000 years. It is verily the age of iron. Everything—the elements, the duration of life, the character of mankind—has deteriorated from the golden years of Satyug. This degeneration . . .' he paused for breath, coughed, cleared his throat, and indelicately spat out the phlegm somewhere in the vicinity of the mike, 'this degeneration will, must, continue and increase until the end of the yug. Verily is it said, "The land shall lose its fertility, the rain shall not fall from the clouds, the cows will yield but little milk."

'When the end of the world approaches, Kalki will come astride a pale horse and put an end to this confusion of sin and pain. Lord Vishnu, it is said by those who know, will appear in his tenth and final avataar. He will appear as Kalki. Handsome and a king among men, he will be armed with a huge axe; his voice will resemble the rolling of thunder, the noise of which will spread terror everywhere. First he will destroy all kings, then all other men. Finally, seeing that his father and mother are but sinners like the rest of mankind, he will sacrifice them also to appease his anger. After this a New Age will begin, when, once again, virtue and happiness will reign on the earth.'

I listened riveted to the apocalyptic vision. 'Kalki,' I

sighed to myself and thought of the white horse with a mane like the hair of an old woman, weaving and wandering through the pall of dust and diesel, and of the desolate crowds by the lottery stalls. 'Of course, his name must be Kalki.'

TWENTY-FOUR

I worried incessantly about when I would encounter Kalki again. My face had sprouted a crop of uncharacteristic pimples. I anxiously consulted Phoolwati, who had an answer and solution for everything.

'Use gram flour,' Phoolwati advised sagaciously. 'Gram flour in milk or cream improves the complexion.'

I looked doubtful. 'Why, even the shastras say so,' she said righteously, looking to Lila for confirmation. Lila maintained her usual inscrutable silence. We had almost forgotten what her voice sounded like.

'I'll come to the temple with you,' I told Phoolwati. I was eager to meet Pandit Kailash Shastry and discover more about Kalki.

Pandit Kailash Shastry was in a very mellow mood. He had correctly predicted the birth of a grandson to a leading jeweller of Old Delhi. The octogenarian grandfather was so overjoyed by the pandit's prognostications that he had decided to endow our temple with a gold-plated cupola.

Phoolwati was ecstatic. 'Wah-wah! It will look just like

the Taj Mahal then!' she said, a visionary look in her eyes. 'Your Ammi was a great saint, Gudiya; she has showered wealth on this temple and all her devotees.'

'The Taj Mahal, too, was once a Hindu palace,' the pandit pronounced.

'Now you forget about palace-walace,' Phoolwati said impatiently, 'and tell me about my Gudiya's future.'

I was tired of questioning him on the subject, for he always fobbed me off with murmurs of 'not now, not just yet'. Today, however, to my surprise, he readily agreed to Phoolwati's request.

'The time has arrived,' he said, smiling inscrutably, 'to look into our Gudiya's future.'

Pandit Kailash Shastry decided to cast my new horoscope according to the horological method, by the astrological positions prevalent at the time the question was posed. He extracted a gold pen from his pocket and scribbled furiously, muttering to himself as he did so. Phoolwati and I waited patiently, unable to construe his little snorts and exclamations. After he had finished, he was silent for a while. Then, after rolling his eyes and murmuring 'Hari Om' a few times, he smiled and fell silent again, as though in a deep trance.

Both Phoolwati and I were wise to these well-known atmospheric tricks and urged him to get on with it. But he was not to be hurried and remained maddeningly quiet.

'How old are you, Gudiya?' he asked at last. I wanted to correct him, to point out that I was not Gudiya but Pooja, but Phoolwati nudged me to remain silent and replied on my behalf.

'Now this is a question you are better qualified to answer, Panditji,' she said. 'After all, are you the astrologer or am I? If I were the astrologer, and you were Phoolwati, I would be occupying these premises and you would be running the shop outside.'

Pandit Kailash Shastry was not in the least amused. He fixed a piercing look upon me and awaited my reply.

'I was eight when we left the haveli,' I said, 'or was it six?' I bit my tongue as I realized the slip, but they seemed not to have noticed. The pandit was muttering something about the balance of dashas at birth, while Phoolwati looked complacent about her cutting wit.

'I am seventeen,' I declared, deciding to choose my age as arbitrarily as my name. Phoolwati protested and began making calculations that ranged from the year of Shambhu's death to the onset of my womanhood, but I pinched her and she fell silent.

Panditji cleared his throat and began. 'Fortune will follow you wherever you go,' he said impressively, 'and not only that, but constant good luck and the blessings of elders.' I listened impatiently; I had heard it all before.

'You have a secret enemy,' he continued portentously. 'He will try to harm you, yet face to face he will smile and act like a friend!' An ant was crawling over his white kurta in the direction of his collar.

He let the warning sink in. I was not unduly alarmed; I had heard the routine a million times before. A 'secret enemy', a 'cunning woman', a 'jealous friend' were all recurring and monotonous motifs in his auguries, usually prompting a hurried confidence about their possible identities from his clients. This was followed by an unsubtle hint from the pandit to the effect that the impediment could be expeditiously removed from the devotee's horoscope by the payment of a suitable sum of money.

But surely he could not have any such financial motive here! I was after all my grandmother's granddaughter! How dare he treat me like an ordinary client!

'However, as you are the granddaughter of my guru, it is my duty to ensure that no harm will ever befall you. After the next new moon, I shall present you with an amulet which shall guard you against such machinations,' he said.

He closed his eyes again and his brows wrinkled in concentration, as if he was wrestling with an impossible mathematical problem. Then he consulted his red cloth-bound panchang and seemed perceptibly cheered by whatever he read there.

'Fame, name, and good fortune,' he repeated again, as though it were a mantra. Again a pause. He was being simply infuriating. I got up to leave, but he motioned me to remain seated.

'The lord of the ascendant is in the second and the lord of the second is in the eleventh house, while the house of the eleventh is in the first,' he said. 'Do you realize what that means?'

We confessed that we did not.

'Gold, a lot of gold, will come your way,' he exclaimed. I was startled, but tried not to betray my reaction. He shut his eyes again as though lost in a trance.

'There is a gaja-kesari yoga,' he continued. 'You will inherit an old woman's money. You will be a rich woman!

Wealth will march to your door like an elephant in heat!' The ant had crawled all the way up his collar and was now poised on the folds of his angavastram.

I was enjoying myself now. I was sure he was right, all this anticipable good fortune was the very least life owed to Pooja Abhimanyu Singh. 'And that's not all! The moon in the seventh is aspected by Jupiter, Sun, and Mercury. That indicates an early marriage!'

Phoolwati's face was wreathed in smiles. 'With your blessings, Panditji,' she said gratefully. 'But what about her health? And will the boy be rich ? From a good family?'

'To gain something, you have to lose something. There is a karmic balance in our deeds. Always, but always, your grandmother is there to protect you. But remember, even in the other world, she could be distracted, busy with some devotee. In such a moment, if you too forget your grandmother and the samskaras she has taught you, then there is grave danger.'

Phoolwati was satisfied. 'Thank you, Panditji, and now I must get going,' she said, lumbering to her feet. 'I had left the dal cooking on the pot, and I am sure it has got burnt!'

I still had a question. 'Do you have any spells or potions, any tantric knowledge, that can make a person fall in love with another person?' I asked, as subtly as I could.

Phoolwati burst out laughing. 'You silly girl, if he knew these arts, don't you think he would use them for himself? No wife, no children, total Brahmacharya! What does he know of these things? Ask me, you madcap, ask me! I could teach you a thing or two!'

And she flounced out, saucily swinging her braid and bestowing a coquettish smile on the pandit as she left.

TWENTY-FIVE

Ever since grandmother died, Lila had attached herself, like a silent smiling piece of statuary, to the same spot near the samadhi where she had settled herself after the burial. She had not abandoned her post even for a day. She was losing weight rapidly, and her salt and pepper hair had turned almost entirely grey. Some afternoons she got up, her legs stiff and unsteady from the unusual exertion, and waddled over to hear Phoolwati's musical exertions.

One evening I witnessed an extraordinary occurrence. Phoolwati was 'indisposed', her recalcitrant gastric juices had played up again and Pandit Kailash Shastry had gone to his hometown in Uttar Pradesh for an overnight visit. A small crowd of devotees waited patiently in the courtyard, accustomed as they were to delays and changes in schedule. Lila shuffled up to the dais and sat down next to the mike, as she used to when grandmother was alive.

I wondered if she was suffering from a memory lapse. Perhaps her mind was harking back to the old days, when she had sat there as grandmother's faithful shadow.

A faltering, uncertain expression rippled across her face, and her features arranged themselves uncertainly into another pattern altogether. There before me shone Ammi's face—her sane, wise, practical, sceptical face! No one else had noticed the transformation; they just continued to sit around, staring at her incuriously as they waited for Phoolwati or the pandit to turn up.

Lila looked earnestly at her audience. 'Beloved brothers and sisters,' she said tentatively. 'I am here today because the spirit of our late revered Mataji has communicated some very important messages to me. Yes, Mataji herself has instructed me . . .' and here her voice changed and became uncannily like Ammi's, 'not to forget her. She speaks from the hereafter. She has described heaven, swarga, to me. She says it is a very nice place; the weather is very pleasant, not hot and dusty like our Delhi. The people are all very beautiful, tall and fair and graceful, rather like our Gudiya. The air is clear and the food is good, although of course they don't need to eat anything there. It's only for the taste, if you get what I mean, sometimes a mango, sometimes a mithai.'

The audience was listening to her intently.

'She has told me to remind you—this is her message— that everything is transient, everything passes, everybody dies, but it makes no difference because life continues. Even after death everything changes, but everything continues . . . '

At this point something happened to Lila. She lost her nerve, and her features abruptly rearranged themselves into their old familiar pattern, and she rushed off the dais in some confusion.

A few women from the audience ran after her, their faces

shining with ecstasy. 'She has returned,' they exclaimed, 'Our Mataji is back!'

Lila sat down quietly at her post near grandmother's samadhi. The women followed her there. They touched her feet reverentially and sought her blessings, but she ignored them completely, rather, I thought to myself, like grandmother might have done.

When I returned to Phoolwati's and described what had happened, she was most indignant. 'That impostor!' she exclaimed. 'So now she's harbouring ambitions, is she?'

I told her that in my opinion Lila was simply going crazy from sitting in the same place all the time. She was just a harmless old woman, and Phoolwati was being unnecessarily harsh on her.

'That's what you think,' Phoolwati replied, her breasts heaving vehemently. 'You don't understand the implications!'

Upon his return the next day, Pandit Kailash Shastry was alerted to the new development. He was not unduly perturbed.

'Theek hai, it's all right,' he said calmly. 'There is a meaning in everything. Let me consult the Prasna Tantra. I must examine the ninth house. Who knows? Perhaps . . .'

'Don't tell me you're going senile as well,' Phoolwati said scornfully. 'Come, Gudiya, let's return home; your grandmother just appeared before me in a vision and told me it's time we had our lunch!'

Phoolwati grumbled incessantly about Lila's insufferable presumption and prevailed upon Pandit Kailash Shastry to persuade her that these visions were somehow sacrilegious. Lila did not appear on the dais again, but she continued her vigil besides grandmother's grave, her white hair tied into a tight bun, her face wreathed in a beatific smile.

As for me, I was cautiously transforming from Gudiya to the self-born identity of Pooja Abhimanyu Singh. I spent a lot of time conceptualizing Pooja, her background, her family, her past and, naturally, her future.

I decided that Pooja had been switched at birth by a careless hospital attendant. The other child, the actual Gudiya, was growing up, surrounded by comfort and luxury, in her ancestral home. Her doting parents complied with her every wish, little realizing that she was nothing but a changeling, while the real Pooja Abhimanyu Singh languished in Phoolwati's hut, deprived by cruel fate of her true heritage.

My daydreaming did not end there. I was convinced that Ammi had known about the switch, perhaps, for some sinister reason, even initiated it. The gold coin that lay hidden in my trunk was, to my dreaming mind, further proof of my true identity. When the time came I would confront my blood parents and claim the life which was legitimately mine.

I spent hours examining the photograph of my 'father', the one I had appropriated from the junk shop whose kabadhi owner was Phoolwati's friend. I had the photograph set in an elaborate gilt frame and after carefully examining the fading sepia tints decided that the man with the thin mouth and cruel smile was incontrovertibly my estranged father—Thakur Abhimanyu Singh. The Thakur lived in feudal splendour in his palace in Rajasthan, tended to by the insipid and obedient Gudiya, quite unaware of the fact that his aristocratic bloodline was condemned to the bizarre guardianship of Phoolwati and Pandit Kailash Shastry.

As Pooja, I had even begun to find the smell in Phoolwati's hut unbearable. I had never really noticed it earlier—the compound of food smells and body warmth had been a part of daily life and sometimes even a relief from the cloying incense and marigold odours of the temple. Now suddenly these same smells reeked of poverty and social suppression. I resented my surroundings intensely and longed to somehow break out into a new life.

Kalki was always in my thoughts. He intrigued and fascinated me. I took to strolling casually outside the row of shops that housed the Shiv Mohan Band, but he was never to be sighted. I screwed up the courage to ask one of his fellow-musicians about Kalki. The fact that I didn't know his real name confused matters. The musician (he played the clarinet) looked blank and, after asking me a number of complicated questions, shrugged indifferently and said he really did not know who I was talking about.

Pandit Kailash Shastry announced his intent to build a suitable memorial for grandmother. He showed us a sketch that the sculptor had forwarded. Ammi was seated in the lotus posture with one hand raised in benediction. The marble had been ordered from Makrana and the statue was to be unveiled by an important local politician whom the pandit had been carefully cultivating.

After the evening aarti was over and Phoolwati's disco bhajans with their rap-like beat had left her audience quite exhausted, the pandit took the mike and exhorted the devotees to generously contribute towards the new monument. 'It is time for all of us to assertively protect our dharma,' he said stentorially, 'and I would appeal to all of you to participate in setting up a fitting memorial to the living saint it was our good fortune to encounter. Great punya will accrue to all of your who do so and Mataji's blessings will lighten the burden of life in Kalyug!'

A steel donation box with a combination lock was displayed prominently on the platform and the pandit kept a close watch on the devotees who filed past it on their way out, bestowing approving smiles on the realized souls who obligingly bent over and dropped their money in.

Phoolwati, already privy to the number of the combination lock, insisted on keeping a duplicate key to the safe. 'Just in case,' she insisted. 'It's safer to have two keys, just in case.'

'Just in case what?' Pandit Kailash Shastry asked.

'You know,' she replied evasively. But she had her way and added the key to the bunch that dangled provocatively from a knot in her sari pallav.

TWENTY-SIX

One Monday, feigning a headache, I didn't go to school. I did not really have to take the trouble of putting up an excuse, for Phoolwati was quite lax about academic life, not having forgiven Roxanne for trying to annex me. 'No good comes of these studies-wuddies,' she would say. 'Why, look at me!'

I intended to spend the day trying out a new hairstyle I had seen in a film magazine. Phoolwati had developed an insatiable addiction for the more lurid species of film gossip, and we subscribed to a number of publications devoted to the Bombay film industry. Her friend the kabadhi also supplied us with back numbers of these magazines, and the hut was piled high with brightly coloured copies of *Stardust*, *Movie* and *Filmi Duniya*.

Since Phoolwati was almost completely illiterate, it fell to me to read aloud the more salacious gossip to her. Then we would sit down and examine the pictures together. 'So that's her, is it?' Phoolwati would exclaim righteously. 'Who would imagine that such an innocent looking girl could break up another woman's marriage? No good will come of it!'

After we had exhausted the month's quota of available gossip and longingly examined the opulent interiors of the film stars' houses, Phoolwati set off for her shop, while I conducted a meticulous update on the life and times of the film star Pooja, the selfsame one who had inspired me to change my name and identity.

Just as I had got down to the business of the new hairstyle, there was a knock on the door. Kalki was standing outside. He was as handsome as ever, but there was a sheepish, even embarrassed, look on his face.

'Where were you?' I asked him. I was half-way through my coiffure, it had been backcombed until it stood on end, and the bangs on my forehead had been trimmed into a winsome fringe.

'Oh, here and there,' he said airily. 'I'm not a person who can stay in one place for long. I went to try my luck!'

Some woman's instinct instructed me to remain cool. 'Weren't you in Delhi, then?' I asked, with a brave show of indifference.

Kalki didn't reply. He was examining the framed photograph of my father. He scrutinized the aristocratic face, the cold smile and the thin lips.

'My father,' I said, in a studiedly casual tone. 'My mother's dead.'

'I thought Phoolwati was your mother,' Kalki said.

His words smote my heart. Stricken with shame and humiliation, I looked around at my mean surroundings, at the cow-dung floor, the makeshift windows boarded with ply, the enormous double bed that straddled the room and the filmi posters that plastered the walls. How was he to know?

'What about your parents?' I asked defensively, for he had not so far displayed any signs of possessing a family. 'Don't you have any relatives?'

'You could say that I'm on my own,' he replied evasively.

'The pandit says that your name is Kalki. Is that true?'

He looked surprised, then pleased. 'Yes, sure, why not, it's Kalki.'

'I'm not really Gudiya, but Pooja Abhimanyu Singh,' I continued.

'Hello, Pooja,' he said in English, extending his hand. 'How do you do?'

'How do you do, Kalki?' I replied, and we shook hands.

His face was very close to mine. His eyes were so intense I was sure they could see all the way through to my soul. My insides were all a flutter. I could hardly breathe. I thought that he would kiss me, but he didn't.

'I went to Bombay,' he said, looking away, as though he had lost interest in me. 'I went to meet a music director there.'

'What happened?' I asked.

'He wasn't in Bombay,' he replied.

We were interrupted by Sundar, who had come in search of Phoolwati. He glared at Kalki and asked me gruffly why I hadn't gone to school.

Kalki got up to leave. 'I'll be seeing you then,' he said.

'No, you won't,' Sundar Pahalwan interrupted. 'Not if you know what's good for you.' He directed a threatening grimace at Kalki and stomped out, slamming the door behind him.

Kalki pulled a mocking face and strolled out with a slow and studied insolence. Manifestly he did not know what was good for him, for the very next evening he was back again.

'Come with me,' he said. 'Will you?' His eyes held a manic intensity, they were almost popping out of their sockets.

I agreed unhesitatingly. We went first to the headquarters of the Shiv Mohan Band. Kalki changed into his gold and braid uniform. He wore epaulettes on his shoulders. He had bought himself new shoes.

'I'm taking you to a marriage party,' he said proudly.

I examined my own worn out salwar suit. I should have changed my clothes.

'I'll be back in a few minutes,' I told him.

He grabbed the drummer by the wrist and checked the time on his watch. 'I give you five minutes,' he said impatiently.

I rushed home and rummaged through my clothes. I had nothing to wear. I took out the old tin trunk and found one of Ammi's odhnis. It was a shimmering blue-green length of chiffon softly sequinned with gold and silver. I draped it over my salwar kameez and rushed out, praying that I wouldn't bump into Phoolwati on the way.

By the time I returned the band had reassembled. They were a motley lot, and in the fading half-light they looked discouraged and dispirited. Their uniforms were shabby; a miasma of grime and decay sat upon them. Some of them were huddled in a group, gossiping and taking quick, nervous puffs at noxious smelling beedis. The clarinet player poked the drummer in the ribs and winked meaningfully when he saw me.

Kalki was looking heartbreakingly handsome. He was standing apart from the rest of the crowd, a soft smile on his fine lips, his large dreamy eyes looking both amused and sad. He had flicked his hair back, and I thought he looked more handsome than any film star.

The band had been commissioned to lead a wedding procession. We made our way in a straggly single file, past the backlanes of our colony to the traffic lights, where the wedding party was to assemble.

'It's to be a really grand wedding,' the drummer told me importantly. We waited forlornly by the traffic lights until two caparisoned elephants, four camels, and eight horses joined us. Then the wedding coach arrived—a huge, throne-like rath surrounded by flashing lights, with its own captive power-generator. The band struck up a lively tune, and as the turbaned groom, in his shining cloth-of-gold achkan, alighted from his flower bedecked car and clambered atop the chariot, the gaiety and excitement caught up with me.

Six orange-turbaned men wearing angarakhas, holding up flaming torches in their hands, led the way. They were followed by a dozen men in the Shiv Mohan Band's gold and braid uniform, holding gas lamps atop their heads. Then, at a safe distance, came the elephants, followed by the camels, the horses, the band, and finally, the bridegroom's chariot.

This was followed by a motorcade of some twenty cars carrying the members of the bridegroom's family. All the cars were large and flashy and profusely decorated with flowers and balloons.

I had no choice but to walk with the band. The gas lamps and the flashing neon lights on the groom's chariot threw an incandescent light, rather like a halo, around Kalki's face. All about us there was a great hooting of traffic, and rows of stalled cars and rickshaws and irate passengers waited for us to pass. Kalki was playing the trombone, his face red with exertion, and he was sweating very slightly on the forehead.

I longed to wipe off the beads of perspiration, but we were walking very fast, in time to the music, and I found it difficult to break out of the beat.

The baraatis had organized a display of fireworks at the next crossing. There was a dazzling burst of anars and ghanchakkars and rockets. As the fluorescent blue and green lights streaked through the night, there was a sudden moment of panic. Disturbed by the fireworks, one of the elephants turned back, upsetting the camels and frightening the horses, who began rearing and neighing nervously. There was a smell of cordite in the air. Panic spread through the wedding procession, and the band stopped midway.

I turned to Kalki. Handing me his trombone, he rushed ahead and began comforting and calming the horses. The elephant looked around, and, reassured, resumed leading the way with its heavy majestic tread. The moment of panic passed, and the festivities began again.

We proceeded in a disorderly way to the park where the marriage feast was to be held. Magnificent illumined gates decorated with flowers and bunting had been erected to welcome us. Women in rich brocade saris, aglitter with jewellery, were waiting for the bridegroom's arrival. They washed his feet ritually with a pitcher of milk, while the band played a sentimental Hindi film song. Then the conductor, Shiv Mohan himself, instructed us to disperse until further notice, for a quartet of shehnai players had been specially invited to perform. *continuation of fairy tale theme*

We wandered around the marriage grounds, examining the fairy-tale decorations. Rows of coloured lights were strung over the trees and bushes. The tapestried tents were illumined with chandeliers. There were colourful carpets and gilt and velvet chairs. The night was awash with the smells of mogra and jasmine. A waiter sidled up with a trayful of cool drinks. I graciously accepted a cola. Kalki discovered a small booth where a select few were discreetly being served rum and whisky. He befriended the waiter, and after he had quickly downed a few, and his eyes were a little more bloodshot and intense than usual, he pushed me behind some bushes and began kissing me fervently.

He ripped open my kurta and fondled me with fierce passion. He pummelled my breasts until I cried with pain, and then moved his attentions downwards. When he entered me I let out a fierce cry of pain. He put his hand over my mouth and told me untenderly to shut up, didn't I know there were people around?

He buttoned up his gold-braided maroon trousers and swaggered out, while I sat huddled behind the bushes in my torn kurta. I listened to the sounds of merriment around me. Then the band began to play, and I thought I could hear the sounds of Kalki's trombone through the din. Next there was a clatter of plates as the guests began to eat, and the delicious smells of tikkas and tandoori chicken. I was ravenously hungry, but my stomach was contracting with an even more powerful desire, and I knew that I was irrevocably in love.

After a while Kalki appeared with a plateful of food. He had been drinking again, the sweetish smells of cheap liquor sat on his breath. After I had eaten, he kissed me again, and then he fumbled for the drawstring of my pyjamas. This time I experienced the full glory of sex, I shuddered with absolute convulsions of ecstasy, and he had to put his hand to my mouth to stop my moans.

When we were finished he wore a satisfied smile on his face. 'Liked it?' he asked complacently. 'Girls always do.'

We had to wait for the guests to leave before I could emerge from behind the bushes. We crept out after the lights had dimmed, and there was only the monotonous clatter of the hired urchins cleaning the piled-up plates in enormous tin tubs.

I wrapped the sequinned blue-green odhni tightly around me to hide my torn kurta. The midnight streets were quite deserted. When I reached home, Phoolwati was securely asleep, a bottle of cough syrup nestling near her pillow. She had locked the door, and I had to clamber in through the window, which had a loose catch I knew how to manipulate.

Phoolwati turned around and examined me groggily. 'So you're back, are you,' she mumbled, and dozed off again. I crept into bed, maintaining a fastidious distance from her, and stayed awake all night reliving what had happened.

TWENTY-SEVEN

When I awoke Phoolwati was perched at the foot of my bed, staring at me quizzically. The chiffon odhni was still wrapped around me, and I could see her gaze fixed on the telltale tear on my kurta, through which my firm breasts were peeping out with a decided air of guilt.

'So,' she said ominously, 'you were in a hurry, were you?'

I pulled up the coverlet and pretended to be asleep, but she was not to be fooled.

'Don't try any sweet untruths; just tell me how far you've gone,' she hissed. Her eyes held mine, and her warm plump hand clasped firmly at my wrist. She pulled me up and pinched me furiously on the cheek, anger and exasperation mingling with concern. 'Your grandmother handed me the responsibility of bringing you up, and no one can say that Phoolwati goes back upon her responsibilities.'

'I don't know what you're talking about,' I protested ineffectually, 'truly, I don't.'

'Just let that motherfucker show me his face, and then see how Phoolwati fixes him,' she said through clenched teeth.

Then her essentially practical nature surfaced. 'Well, what can't be cured must be endured,' she murmured with sudden equanimity. 'And who knows? He might be a very nice boy after all! He looks like a film star all right! Whatever you do, your grandmother's blessings are always with you. Who knows?' She smiled optimistically, and, after several exhortations on the values of womanly virtue and modesty, set off for the shop, commanding me to remain at home until she returned.

She came back in the afternoon, escorted by Sundar Pahalwan. They had Kalki in tow. He looked lost and abashed and even a little scared.

Sundar twirled his moustache, flexed his biceps and gave Kalki two resounding slaps, one on each cheek, which sent him reeling. I cried out in protest, but Phoolwati gave me a quick, hard pinch to silence me.

Kalki had fallen to the floor. He got up, his faced flushed with anger and shame and the impact of Sundar's slap.

'Go touch the feet of your future mother-in-law!' Sundar Pahalwan instructed him.

Kalki knelt down and submissively touched Phoolwati's pink-painted toenails.

'What about your mother?' Sundar continued, twirling his moustache to a fine point. 'I'm sure even you have one! Does she happen to remember who your father might have been?'

Kalki sprang to his feet. His face was white with anger. He clenched his fists and pummelled ineffectually at Sundar's massive frame. Sundar smiled, complacently massaged his bulging muscles and knocked Kalki down with a casual, deliberate arrogance. Blood spouted from Kalki's nose. I rushed to where he lay, cossetting his head on my lap, wiping the ooze from his face and kissing him.

Phoolwati was fussing over Sundar, who was acting modestly heroic. Kalki lay still on my lap for some time, then he struggled to his feet. 'What do you want me to do?' he asked Sundar.

'Marry Gudiya,' Sundar Pahalwan replied.

'And soon,' Phoolwati added.

Kalki shrugged. 'Okay,' he said. 'I don't mind.' He looked at me. Anger and hatred gleamed in his eyes.

We were engaged the next afternoon in the temple compound. It was a simple ceremony. Pandit Kailash Shastry officiated. Phoolwati and Sundar did the honours. Kalki came accompanied by Shiv Mohan of the Shiv Mohan Band.

Later, Pandit Kailash Shastry voiced his doubts. 'My reservations are not merely astrological,' he said. 'I simply don't think that he is a very nice person. Besides, who and where are his family? What is his surname, or even his name for that matter, leave alone his gotra!'

'But you told me he was called Kalki,' I pointed out.

'That was only a metaphor,' Pandit Kailash Shastry sighed. 'I don't think you should marry him, Gudiya.'

Kalki's behaviour had changed after our engagement. He was surprisingly subdued and decorous. He was studiously polite and maintained an elaborate distance from me. I longed for his touch, but our infrequent meetings were diligently chaperoned by Phoolwati, and there was never any scope for intimacy or tenderness.

'We could have a double wedding,' Phoolwati said to me

dreamily one day. I found the idea grotesque. Besides I had not forgiven Sundar for the thrashing he had given Kalki. Phoolwati and Sundar were becoming more juvenile by the day in the display of their passion. She wrote him absurd love letters, which she would dictate to me, for she didn't know how to put pen to paper. He would reciprocate by sending her audio cassettes of Hindi films with suggestive titles. In the course of the evening bhajans, which Sundar now regularly attended, Phoolwati would make arch references to Krishna and Radha, or Shiva and Parvati, and throw languishing looks at Sundar from the dais. I found it all distasteful in the extreme and considered it a quite different quality of emotion from my love for Kalki.

There was still very little that I knew about Kalki. I was sure that, once we were married, my undemanding love would lower the defences he had built around himself and that one day we would achieve some sort of harmony with each other. He continued to maintain an impenetrable facade of gracious and strained dignity. The camaraderie, the unspoken bond, that had brought us together might never have existed. I had lost his trust.

Time and again Pandit Kailash Shastry remonstrated Phoolwati for our rash shotgun engagement. 'Astrological suppositions apart,' he said, 'how could you even think of hitching up our Gudiya with that uneducated lout? It can never be.'

Phoolwati spat out fragments of the paan leaf she was chewing. 'And if his little worm were to crawl into her belly, and leave her with a baby in her lap, what will you and I do then, Panditji,' she asked, her massive bosom heaving with emotion.

Pandit Kailash Shastry blushed to the roots of his hair. 'That's true,' he conceded, and returned to the study of the Prashna Tantra.

I was slowly eliciting whatever information I could from the circle of Kalki's acquaintances. The clarinet player, Kedar, was an inveterate gossip. I gathered that Kalki was an orphan. He was also, Kedar implied, a bastard. His father had been a Nepali and his mother a maidservant. They had lived together without benefit of matrimony until the Nepali's first wife came back to him, whereupon Kalki's mother was discarded and subsequently she died.

Mr Shiv Mohan confirmed the story. 'Kalki has never forgiven his parents for abandoning him,' he said. 'But don't ever tell him that I told you all this. I love the boy as though he were my own son. There's something about him, a kind of rage, that reminds me of myself when I was a boy.'

Thereafter a bond was forged between us. Both Shiv Mohan and I felt somehow compelled to look after Kalki, to protect him, obscurely, from himself. 'The troubles he has caused me,' Mr Shiv Mohan sighed, toying restlessly with the big brass buttons on his red and gold coat, 'anybody else would have fired him. But then, there's something about him.'

TWENTY-EIGHT

Life in the temple continued much as before. Our new prosperity was heralded by the arrival of a desert cooler, which Sundar wired up in Phoolwati's hut. He had already stolen an electricity wire from the main pole, and we now had an unlimited supply of free power. We no longer had to wait for the monsoon breezes to come and revive us; the summer was endurable at the touch of a button.

As for the pandit, he was prospering in every way. People flocked to him from all over the city for astrological consultations. There was even a foreigner, a German woman named Maria Smetacek, who spent long hours alone with him. All of us regarded her with consuming curiosity. He insisted that she was merely his disciple and that she was undertaking a study of the Indian system of astrology. She was an unattractive woman with large teeth and a sad and serious face.

Phoolwati and I were immensely intrigued. A foreigner in our temple. It gave the place another dimension altogether. 'These men are all the same,' Phoolwati declared. 'Mark my words, this panditua will bring shame and ruination to our temple by his activities.'

That was not all. The pandit had become so rich that he was thinking of buying himself a car. Phoolwati was not doing too badly either, for more visitors to the temple naturally meant more customers at her shop. Some other entrepreneurs had tried to move in and put up their own stalls and kiosks outside the premises, but Sundar Pahalwan had nipped their efforts in the bud.

'He broke every bone in their legs,' Phoolwati announced with proud satisfaction. 'Every single bone! Now he's what I call a real man—not like that Shambhu!' A fond smile wreathed her face, and she belched contentedly, then fell into a little reverie.

I looked around, and examined the changes in Phoolwati's room. The transformation around us was little short of miraculous. An enormous television set with an accompanying video player sat proudly on an aluminium and plastic trolley, and two sparkling new steel cupboards occupied the little remaining space.

One afternoon, as I was sitting on our king-sized bed, bemusedly contemplating our fast-expanding possessions, Phoolwati sprang to her feet and leapt to the corner that held the steel cupboards. She possessed the extraordinary agility that characterises many fat people, and I was always surprised anew by the lithe grace of her enormous body. She unlocked the steel cupboards, busily selecting the keys from the jangling bunch that hung from her sari pallav, and flung them open.

'Come, Gudiya, see what Phoolwati has to show you,'

she said excitedly, and extracted a fistful of hundred rupee notes. 'This is nothing,' she boasted, her face aglow with childlike enthusiasm, 'there's more where it came from. It's from my partnership with Sundar! Your Phoolwati is a rich woman now, and you can tell your precious Kalki that!'

The grimy bank notes were stapled into four thick wads. I was impressed, for I had never actually seen so much money before. Life was full of surprises. It was as if some benevolent djinn had granted that all our wishes come true. As predicated in the fairy stories my Ammi used to tell me, I had found a handsome prince. Phoolwati too seemed on the verge of getting hers. But I knew that this was not strictly accurate; our love remained in the realm of make-believe, for, behind his carefully maintained facade, Kalki was seething with a desperate rage. He had in no way forgiven me for our engagement. Whatever I did, I simply could not penetrate his hatred.

I sighed deeply, reflecting on life's ironies. Phoolwati looked concerned. 'What's bothering my Gudiya?' she asked worriedly, still waving the wads of notes in her podgy hands. 'Arre, Gudiya, you are born to be a princess—you have your grandmothers blessings. Tell Phoolwati what you want, Gudiya, and she will get if for you. Just test your Phoolwati for once.'

I was so touched by her concern that I even forgave her for calling me 'Gudiya' instead of 'Pooja'.

'Tell me what's worrying you, Gudiya Rani,' she cajoled. 'I promised your dead grandmother that I would look after you. You wanted that wretch Kalki, and you got him! Whatever happens, I will keep my promise. Now tell me, why are you sad?'

'How can I explain, Phoolwati,' I sighed. 'I never thought that being in love could make a person unhappy.'

'Are you talking about that Zero-Hero?' she asked contemptuously. 'I wish you had fallen in love with a real man, Gudiya.'

'I love Kalki,' I said irritably. 'And my name is Pooja. Why can't you remember that?'

'How I wish you could have married a rich man,' she continued wistfully. 'Rich men are different.'

I pointed out that the only rich man she had ever remotely known was the zamindar for whom her mother worked. She impatiently dismissed my objection.

'I know Sundar,' she said. 'And if he isn't rich, then your name isn't Gudiya.'

'How rich?' I asked. 'After all, how rich can somebody like Sundar be?' She immediately forgot about Kalki and launched into a long description of Sundar Pahalwan's multifarious economic activities. Phoolwati was always lucid when she talked about business. As she outlined Sundar's new trucking venture, the ten buffaloes she had advised him to buy and the six shops he had constructed on a vacant piece of disputed land after bribing the municipality officials, I realized that they formed the perfect partnership. Sundar was a very lucky man to have her as an ally.

'So you see, Gudiya Rani,' she said in conclusion, tweaking my cheeks affectionately as she spoke, 'your Phoolwati isn't all that stupid. I'll have a palace of my own, one day, and then you and that wretched Kalki can move in with me.'

I believed her implicitly. If she had so decided, Phoolwati was bound to become a very prosperous woman.

'There's something I want to ask you, Phoolwati,' I said, trying to articulate a puzzle which had vexed me for some time now. 'How is it that all of us—you, me, Panditji and Sundar—are all getting richer and richer? Just some time ago we were all ordinary footpath wallahs! How long will we continue to be so lucky?'

'Arre, these are all your grandmother's blessings, Gudiya,' Phoolwati replied piously. 'Even Panditji was telling me that. Whatever she touched turned to gold. We have her to thank for all this.'

I muttered a fervent plea to my sainted Ammi to bless Kalki and me with some measure of the same good luck and fortune that seemed to surround us in such abundance. My thoughts moved, quite inconsequentially, to my mother and her golden hair before she had gone bald, and I wondered with a shiver whether Phoolwati's superstitious analysis of our good fortune could possibly stand up to reason.

TWENTY-NINE

The statue of grandmother which Pandit Kailash Shastry had commissioned was nearing completion. Phoolwati had accompanied the pandit to the workshop in Rajouri Gardens where the sculptor lived. He had never seen grandmother and was working from the colour photograph of Ammi which had been used for the postcards, with the golden 'Om' emblazoned on them. Lila had also obliged by posing for the sculptor, doing the impersonation of my grandmother, at which she had become so adept. Phoolwati had taken violent exception to this, calling it sacrilegious, shameful and sinful.

However, when she and the pandit went to examine the statue in the studio before giving it their final approval, Phoolwati reported with satisfaction that it was most lifelike. The very marble seemed to breathe, she said, and grandmother looked serene and saintly. I reminded her that Ammi had been bad-tempered, irritable and near senile in her last days. She replied that Kalki's company was making me forget my roots.

There was a great deal of debate about whether

grandmother's eyes were to be portrayed open, gazing at her devotees, or closed, looking, as the pandit put it, inwards to her soul. Phoolwati and the sculptor were agreed that they should be open, but Pandit Kailash Shastry insisted that they remain closed and quoted some obscure Brahmanical authority in support of his views.

Phoolwati retorted that she knew very well what was playing in the pandit's mind. He was simply afraid to have grandmother there with her eyes wide open, for he did not want her to see the fraudulent activities he was up to in her temple, what with foreign women disciples, and worse.

Pandit Kailash Shastry maintained his dignity. 'I am not a Brahmachari, but a mere sadhaka,' he replied. 'Witness the fact that I wear only white robes, not a hypocritical saffron. Maria Smetacek is merely my student. She is a learned and noble lady. However, what would an ignorant widow who runs a flowershop know of discipline and learning?'

His comments infuriated Phoolwati even further, and there was active warfare between them for some time. Panditji gave another disciple the franchise for storing the visitor's shoes and chappals. The charge was a nominal twenty-five paise per item of footwear. The scheme went into operation, complete with steel shoe-racks and plastic tokens, until Sundar Pahalwan exercised his territorial muscle. The disciple vanished overnight, taking his shoe-rack and plastic tokens with him, along with the sandals of some unfortunate devotees.

Panditji retaliated by banning Phoolwati from the new toilet he had installed within the temple compound, forcing her to use the public lavatory near the tea shop. When Ammi and I had first arrived in that lonely stretch of road, there had always been the fields, but the temple was now almost entirely surrounded by construction activity, all in different stages of completion.

The feud between Panditji and Phoolwati did not last long. They were both too sensible not to realize where their essential interests lay, and soon they were on the best of terms again.

Once the statue was completed, Pandit Kailash Shastry set about planning a grand ceremony for its installation. The astrologically auspicious time for the consecration ceremony, the 'Pran Pratishtan', was decided upon after consultations with many other eminent astrologers. There was to be a 'Mahabhoj' and a 'Bhandara', where halva-puri cooked in pure ghee would be served to an estimated two thousand devotees.

Bhurroo and the other lepers came forward with a donation of five thousand and one rupees towards the cost of the Bhandara. The offer met with a mixed reaction. Pandit Kailash Shastry was of the opinion that it was a noble and touching gesture and that it would be churlish to refuse them.

Phoolwati differed with him. 'Have you considered the implications!' she exclaimed agitatedly. 'Bhurroo may be a friend of mine, but still . . . It's tantamount to being served by a leper! Chhi chhi! I don't know about you, but as for myself . . . !' Her face assumed a pious and martyred expression, and she turned to Lila for support.

After her singular appearance on the dais, Lila had returned to her silent vigil, with only her moulding deerskin mat for company. She did not respond to Phoolwati's unspoken query, but continued to wear her trademark expression of blank and peaceable impenetrability.

'What do you think, Lila behn?' Pandit Kailash Shastry asked wearily. The constant sparring with Phoolwati was beginning to tell on his nerves, and a permanent worry-line had settled on his broad forehead.

'You know my views,' Lila replied, in a voice quite different from her usual placid monotone. 'I despise these accursed beggars! If one of them wants to part with his money for a change, why then, in the name of God, grab it!'

Phoolwati's chest stopped heaving; Pandit Kailash Shastry's mouth fell agape. We stood absolutely still, staring astoundedly at each other. There was no scope for doubt. The voice was unmistakably Ammi's.

The set of Lila's face had also inexplicably altered. It was sharper, cannier, more like grandmother's. My hair stood up on end and I clutched fiercely at Phoolwati's sari, as though she was my only link with sanity. She too was similarly affected, and her warm hand clutched at mine with an equal degree of panic.

Pandit Kailash Shastry was more objective. He examined Lila's suddenly unfamiliar face with wary detachment. Then he sat down before her and began gently massaging her feet. 'Do your feet hurt, Mataji?' he asked respectfully.

Lila's face reformulated itself again, returning to its usual benign contours. She trembled slightly, as though awakening from a dream. She was wheezing a little. Her wrinkled face looked very old and tired.

'We were discussing Bhurroo's offer. You know that the beggars want to contribute to the Bhandara,' Pandit Kailash

Shastry said tentatively.

Lila looked blank. Phoolwati snorted in relief. 'Arre, Panditji, do whatever you feel is right,' she giggled. 'Let's grab the money if that's what our Mataji desires!' There was an edge of hysteria in her voice.

It was finally decided that we would accept the donation and that it would be utilized, not for the feeding of bhaktas at the Bhandara but for the construction of a silver-plated canopy for grandmother's statue. Bhurroo and the other lepers were most happy with the compromise and graciously declined the offer of a plaque recording their generosity.

That afternoon I sat down beneath my peepul tree. It had been raining recently, and the beautifully shaped leaves were replete with sap and spirit. Fanned by the breeze, they waved around sinuously, as though pleased with themselves. A deep, long sigh escaped from within the dense boughs. I felt languorous and relaxed and strangely contented, as though my brow was being soothed by some unseen hand. I felt I was a little girl again, nestling in my Ammi's lap, sheltered by the pallav of her sari. I fell into a deep sleep, and when I awoke I was startled to find myself there, alone, in the dusk, as the shadows lengthened.

THIRTY

After much research and learned consultation, Pandit Kailash Shastry finally arrived at a consensus about an auspicious time and date for the installation of grandmother's statue.

A temple committee had been specially elected to coordinate all aspects of the installation. The functionaries of this august body, which included Sundar Pahalwan, Phoolwati, Lila and a few of the more prominent devotees, put in all they had to make the event a success.

Specially engraved invitation cards, on handmade paper, with a Sanskrit invocation embossed in gold lettering, had been ordered. The pandit delivered most of them individually. He even called on Roxanne, to extend a personal invitation, but she was away in Bombay, and Mr Lamba gave him short shrift.

The temple was a hive of activity. There were always dhurries being rolled and unrolled, sandals getting lost and accounts getting bungled. It was, as Phoolwati described it, like the preparation for a marriage feast. The only marriage feast I had ever been to was on the eventful day when Kalki had deflowered me. It had been nothing like this, but of course I could hardly say so to Phoolwati.

At last the great day dawned. The statue was to be brought to the temple from the sculptor's studio in Rajouri Gardens in a specially decorated tempo, accompanied, in the later part of the journey, by the Shiv Mohan Band. Although this quite naturally delighted me, my joy in witnessing my beloved Kalki playing the trombone for my deceased grandmother was marred by an unforeseen, and to my young mind, entirely tragic, circumstance.

Hurt by Kalki's calculated and continued coolness, I had decided, in an effort to arouse his interest, to get my nose pierced. I was convinced that it needed only the dazzle of a diamond on my delicate nostril to move him out of his apathy. The neighbourhood jeweller who Phoolwati patronized pierced my right nostril with a fine gold thread and then inserted a small twig of tulsi to help it heal. But nature decided otherwise and my nose became red and grotesquely swollen. Quite apart from my vanity, which was sorely distressed, I was in the most excruciating agony. I kept my face covered with my chunni, as though I were in purdah.

Phoolwati ignored my embarrassed excuses, and insisted that I participate in the strange procession. I found myself seated in a marigold-bedecked tempo, beside the marble statue of my grandmother, which was draped until the time of the consecration in a shroud of white muslin.

We lurched along through the streets of Delhi, accompanied by grandmother's stony presence. Pandit Kailash Shastry, Sundar Pahalwan and a few other prominent patrons and devotees followed in a line of taxis. The band, which had begun promisingly enough with bhajan tunes and devotional music, soon lapsed into 'Come September' and 'The Baby Elephant Walk'. Sweat was trickling in rivulets down my back, and Phoolwati's 'gas' was perceptibly troubling her. I cursed my grandmother for her improbable sainthood and indulged myself in daydreams of a future life with Kalki, far away from the temple.

By the time we returned, an enormous crowd had gathered by the floral gates which Phoolwati had commissioned. They raised resounding cheers of 'Mataji ki Jai' when they saw the tempo arriving. There was a compounded smell of crushed flower petals, incense, and sweat—a smell I had somehow learnt to associate with religion—which met and mingled with the odours of pure ghee and frying puris from the Bhandara. I covered my face with my chunni and tried my best to keep out of Kalki's sight.

We made our way somehow through the crush of bodies. The statue itself was wheeled along on a makeshift trolley, which had been improvised using the roller skate stands the three beggars used to perambulate in.

The pandit was looking solemn and wise. His white dhoti and kurta were starched stiff as any politician's. A green and gold bordered angavastram was draped around his shoulders. Only the telltale flapping of his dhoti front betrayed his excitement.

The priests washed, bathed and anointed every chakra and organ of the image—the eyes, the mouth, the hands, the navel, the feet. Oil and unguents, honey and milk and ghee were lovingly applied to the marble figure. Fragrant flowers were heaped upon grandmother, and then, finally, huge silver pitchers of Ganga water were poured over her in ablution.

Pandit Kailash Shastry conducted the prayers himself. He was assisted by two other Brahmin priests, neither of whom had ever met my grandmother. The inner temple, the sanctum sanctorum, was crowded with all the familiar faces I had known for so many years.

Grandmother's statue, although a little larger and sturdier in replication than her frail bird-like body, was surprisingly evocative and captured some elusive nuance of her always enigmatic personality. After the Sanskrit chantings—which amused me, for grandmother was always ignorant, and indeed scornful, of the language—Phoolwati played a tape of grandmother's bhajans. Ammi's pure liquid voice suddenly brought alive her remembrance in a way nothing had since her death, and I began to weep. Phoolwati put her arms around me and made sympathetic sounds. I forgot about Kalki, and the disastrous nose ring. For a while I was once again the child Gudiya who had grown up in the shadow of her Ammi.

Pandit Kailash Shastry's foreign student was lamentably absent. The Pandit, and indeed all of us, had felt that the presence of a European would add to the prestige of the function, but Phoolwati informed me that Maria Smetacek had perforce returned to Germany on the expiry of her visa.

There was a last-minute hitch in that the local politician who was to garland grandmother's statue did not turn up. The pandit decided that I was to do the honours. Phoolwati had outdone herself with the garland, which was a masterpiece of fragrant and marvellously braided roses strung with young lotus buds.

Almost tripping over under the weight and size of the huge garland, I walked up to the marble statue, and hastily unburdened the flowers over grandmother's neck. I was acutely aware of Kalki's watching presence somewhere in the audience. Although he had been specially invited to join the committee members on the dais, he had declined the invitation, saying that he preferred to be with the other members of the Shiv Mohan Band.

Grandmother's statue had been bathed in milk and ghee and Ganga jal. It was redolent of incense and saffron, surrounded by offerteries of flowers and coconuts. Something in the mood and moment conjured up memories of the day of Ammi's funeral, when her thin frame had been indecorously lowered into a pit in the earth, before the pounding of coconuts had smashed her skull.

I discovered that my cheeks were wet with tears. I was weeping in sorrow and remembrance. The public at large was very appreciative of my tears, and I was showered with sympathetic murmurs and affectionate hugs from Ammi's devotees as I returned to my seat next to Phoolwati.

After I had garlanded Ammi's statue, Phoolwati, Sundar, Panditji and I were to ceremonially feed one hundred and eleven Brahmins who had been specially invited to the 'Mahabhoj'. The kitchen was then to be thrown open to the public at large for the Bhandara, where a dozen halvais were busily preparing food in gargantuan vessels.

Word had spread in the beggar community, and hundreds of ragged emaciated mendicants had lined up outside the temple and were waiting impatiently for the ceremonies to be over. The high-caste guests, some in dhoties, some in trousers and bush shirts, were seated in neat rows, awaiting the feast, specially prepared by a famous maharaj in asli ghee. But the hungry hordes outside were in no mood for patience. They pushed the devotees aside, trampled on the Brahmins, stormed the kitchens, manhandled the halvais and attacked the food. Supreme chaos reigned for over an hour. Finally, their appetites satisfied, they left the temple without so much as a backward glance at my grandmother, sitting with her legs folded in the lotus posture, her hand raised in benediction.

Pandit Kailash Shastry was completely shaken by the confusion. He retired to his room, muttering something about Kalyug and showering curses on the crowds.

Phoolwati was more composed. She settled herself in a corner and waited amusedly for the confusion to subside. When everyone had left, she took me by the hand and led me to the statue.

'Talk to her, Gudiya,' she whispered encouragingly. 'Tell her what you want. Make a wish. She is your grandmother! Mataji will make sure that you get your heart's desire!'

I looked solemnly at the statue. Only one wish resounded from my heart. 'I want Kalki, grandmother,' I said humbly. 'That's all.'

Grandmother's eyes were closed; she could not see me, but I fancied that a familiar expression of disagreeable contempt flashed through her sculpted serenity. I turned away and stumbled headlong into Kalki. He held out his hand to steady me. Thanking my grandmother for her generosity, I hastily covered up my inflamed nostril with the edge of my chunni, and exposed Kalki to my most beguiling smile.

Kalki seemed very worked up. He clutched at my arm and steered me agitatedly to a corner of the hall. 'I must talk to you, Pooja,' he said urgently. 'It's a matter of life and death.'

I could feel my whole body awakening again at his touch. The chunni had slipped down, revealing my grotesquely swollen nose, but Kalki noticed nothing.

'You have to help me, Pooja,' he said. 'I have been thinking about it for a long time. We have to get out of this! Just look at me!' And he pointed expressively at his grimy red uniform and his shoes, which were, inexplicably, once again shabby and down at heel. 'I'm not meant for this, you know that!'

'Tell me what I should do, Kalki,' I said tenderly.

'Magic!' he replied. 'Tantra! My God, it's so obvious, why didn't it strike me before! Your Panditji . . .' he pointed at Pandit Kailash Shastry, who had not yet recovered from the chaos, and who was looking distraught and puzzled, 'and your grandmother,' (turning his head towards Ammi's marbled presence) 'there's nothing these people don't know! We must ask them—we must learn—the secrets of the universe!'

'The secrets of the universe . . .' I mused.

'I'm not joking, Pooja; you know I'm not joking,' he exclaimed. 'Once we learn all that, there's nothing we can't do!' He was smiling broadly now, his excitement was infectious and I was laughing along with him. 'For instance, there's a particular mantra, I believe the pandit knows it, I'm told your grandmother taught it to him. Once you know this mantra, no one can refuse you! You ask someone, anyone—for their house, their bank account, their daughter—anything, anything at all, and they won't refuse you! Imagine that, Pooja, imagine it!'

I tried very hard to imagine being in possession of such a mantra, but I couldn't. I personally had no belief in the efficacy of magic spells and was more than a little sceptical of the Kailash Shastry's abilities. The pandit himself made no claims to any magical powers. As for his astrology, I knew from experience that the often uncanny accuracy of his 'predictions' came from careful research and observation. Moreover, he structured his utterances with such weighted ambiguity that gullible or troubled minds naturally exposed themselves, prompting a correct diagnosis.

I didn't have the heart to tell Kalki this, and besides I was woman enough to understand that any espousal of rationality or disavowal of magic would swiftly provoke Kalki to retreat back into frigid disinterest.

Instead I gave him a mysterious smile. 'Remember, Kalki, that I am my grandmother's granddaughter! In time—if you are nice to me—I might even teach you what I know!'

Our eyes met, and some ancient magic was restored between us. Phoolwati, who, like my grandmother, had developed eyes at the back of her head, materialized by my side and ushered me away.

In the days that passed, my nose healed, and was restored to its former perfection. The twinkling zircon diamond on my mogul profile gave me immense satisfaction. Moreover, it had the intended effect on Kalki's libido, and he began pursuing me with all the old ardour. I longed to meet him alone, but Phoolwati was a fierce and effective chaperone, and Kalki himself had not recovered from or forgotten Sundar's thrashing. Sly looks and stolen kisses had to suffice for our passion.

Some days after the consecrations of grandmother's statue, Lila announced that she was going on a pilgrimage to the four holy dhams. This statement was met with astonishment, and, in the case of Phoolwati, with a degree of relief. Lila's fleeting and uncanny personality changes unsettled her. Besides, being Phoolwati, she ascribed the very basest of motives to what might well have been a totally innocent phenomenon.

'I don't trust her one bit,' she said, chewing at the Pan Parag she had begun to consume in copious quantities. 'I can tell you from my experience of the world that she's up to something! There's a wicked mind hiding behind that simple face! Mark my words, she'll make a throw for it!'

What 'it' meant was never effectively explained. When Pandit Kailash Shastry expressed his doubts about Lila's ability in practical terms to fend for herself in the course of a long journey, Phoolwati's face lit up. 'Perhaps she'll never come back,' she said hopefully. 'There's always a bright side to everything.'

THIRTY-ONE

Sundar Pahalwan had proposed marriage to Phoolwati. She agreed, but her assent was subject to certain conditions. These were, firstly, that he would build a pucca house for her, the ownership of which would be irrevocably hers, secondly, that he would allow her to continue running her businesses as before and, thirdly, that Sundar Pahalwan was to treat me as their adoptive daughter. The third condition both touched and horrified me, and I found to my surprise that he had agreed unflinchingly to all three stipulations.

Phoolwati wanted the marriage to be performed with due ceremony, with Sundar coming to her house astride a horse, accompanied by a band and a baraat. Here Sundar put his foot down, saying that neither of them were of the age for such 'show-sha-giri'. A simple ceremony at the temple would be more appropriate.

They haggled about this for a while, each adamant about the details of their nuptials. Phoolwati had even negotiated a hefty discount from the Shiv Mohan Band, but this only served to further infuriate Sundar. There was to be no 'band baja' in his wedding, he said firmly. The marriage was almost called off, until Sundar came up with the clinching argument that his henchmen, who would naturally constitute the major part of the baraatis, would inevitably drink and brawl through the wedding procession.

'Will it look nice?' he pleaded, drawing me into the argument. 'Think about it, Gudiya—all those drunken mawallis, arriving at the temple! One of them might pass some remark—it could become a matter of honour—it could even lead to murder!'

Phoolwati was persuaded, and they exchanged garlands at the temple, and took the seven steps round the sacred fire, with Pandit Kailash Shastry officiating.

Sundar Pahalwan came dressed in an achhkan-sherwani. His huge wrestler's frame looked strange, draped in cloth of gold, but he managed to carry off even the resplendent pink turban with a degree of panache. Phoolwati was swathed in a Tanjore sari of dazzling hue and texture. She looked sweaty and excited and triumphant.

Phoolwati had called a mehndi-wali home on the wedding eve. She painted an elaborate trellised pattern of henna leaves on Phoolwati's hands and an intricate design of fierce red henna adorned her feet. The mehndi-wali applied a simple paan-leaf design on my hands as well, but somehow the colour did not take and only a pale but pretty pattern surfaced.

Kalki came dressed in a suit. He had bought himself new shoes, and I thought he looked devastatingly handsome. Phoolwati had taken special trouble to attend to my wardrobe, and I was splendidly turned out in a shimmering pink brocade lehnga-dupatta. She had even bought me a real diamond nose ring, and when the photographer snapped us I gave him my right profile so that he wouldn't miss the diamond. The photographer was a friend of Sundar's, and he told Kalki ingratiatingly that the pair of us looked 'just like film stars'.

This put Kalki in a good mood, and he was unusually affectionate and considerate. He tried to coax and humour me into parting with any magic mantras my Ammi might have taught me, and even gave me an affectionate squeeze on my waist.

Only the immediate temple community had been invited to the wedding. Roxanne Lamba made a point of attending the ceremonies. She came armed with an enormous bouquet of red roses. 'I wish you all the very best in your future life,' she said gently, her myopic eyes taking in the details of Sundar's strange appearance with a degree of surprise. Phoolwati remarked later that her presence had lent a touch of class to the function.

Phoolwati's new house was not far from the temple. It was a pucca two-storey building with all modern amenities. Sundar continued to live in his old lodgings, but spent most of his time in Phoolwati's kothi. He was obviously loaded with money, and although the new house was an illegal structure, not sanctioned by the municipality, no expense had been spared in its construction. It had even more marble than the temple. The floors, walls and staircase all had been covered by expanses of polished white stone, until it looked like a mausoleum, or a vault, or an enormous bathtub.

Phoolwati sought my help in furnishing her dream house.

We went on a wild shopping spree, buying anything and everything that looked expensive, luxurious or colourful. We would return from the shops, dump our buys on the floor and set off again. Together, we combed the streets of Karol Bagh and Lajpat Nagar. When we finally ran out of energy and money, we sat down and unpacked our purchases.

The final result was strange but not unpleasing. Phoolwati's kothi looked like a tropical paradise, a dense forest of plastic foliage crowded with velvet roses and brass statuettes. Every room had scenic wallpaper; the landscapes varied from beachside sunsets to icy mountain lakes. Expensive sofa-sets pushed against lacquered jhoolas, and there were synthetic Kashmiri rugs scattered in every corner.

Phoolwati loved flowers. Although she had been enchanted by all the plastic smuggled-from-Bangkok blooms we had bought from the imported goods stalls in Karol Bagh, she was bitterly disappointed by their lack of fragrance. We set about rectifying matters by buying flagons of Dubai perfumes from the same smugglers and dousing the flowers in them. This didn't work, the perfumes simply evaporated, but we didn't give up. We scoured the streets of Old Delhi for traditional itars and other oil-based perfumes and meticulously set about assigning each artificial flower its own individual fragrance.

Sundar was amused by our activities and did not seem to grudge Phoolwati the enormous expenses which she was incurring. He was a most indulgent husband, and no cost or effort was spared to make Phoolwati happy.

I was constantly surprised by the quantities of money they spent. Roxanne was a very rich woman but the household was run on severe, even parsimonious, lines. Nothing was ever wasted, and there were never any random or whimsical expenses. Phoolwati and Sundar revelled in spending money. It was an activity, valid and complete in itself and yielding its own autonomous pleasure.

When I first saw Sundar, when he came to demand the haftha for our jhuggi from grandmother, he was dressed in a quite ordinary fashion, wearing kurta pyjamas or checked lungis. Now that Phoolwati had taken his wardrobe in hand, his clothes were extravagant celebrations of the sartorial imagination. Phoolwati got most of her inspiration from Hindi films, and Sundar's clothes were modelled on the kind of outfits that filmi villains sported. He swaggered about in checked trousers, red shirts, white shoes, with bulky gold chains and enormous floppy handkerchiefs, which always smelt of sweat, as accesories.

Sundar's favourite polyester shirt had a tiger-striped print. He wore it with a checked cap and brown bell-bottomed trousers. I did not know much about clothes, but I sensed that Sundar Pahalwan's loud and overstated clothes were not what real sahibs wore. Of course, Sundar was not a sahib, but a respected and feared dada with impeccable political and criminal connections. Yet I was beginning to like and even respect him.

Another symptom of Sundar's upward mobility was that he had begun to swear in English. He had, in humbler times, a fabled repertoire of foul abuses, in the most imaginative conjunctions. To be called a 'motherfucker or a 'sisterfucker' by Sundar was to be temperately addressed. These invectives were always couched in Hindi, and used as umbrella-words to categorize items as diverse as furniture and footwear. Now, urged on to be a gentleman by Phoolwati, he had abandoned his mother tongue as a vehicle of abuse and graduated to indiscriminately preceding every utterance with a 'bloody bastard'. Thus, we had a bloody bastard truck which wouldn't start, a bloody bastard shoe which didn't fit and a bloody bastard chapatti which had gone cold by the time it left the kitchen.

'But what does Sundar do?' I asked Phoolwati once. 'How does he make so much money?'

She was not offended by my question and enthusiastically launched into a resume of Sundar's business activities. Primarily, of course, he collected protection-money from a dominion of four slums. He lent out this money at exorbitant rates of interest and the appropriated the assets of reluctant customers. He also acted as a factor, buying any bad debts and collecting them with the help of his burly henchmen. Then there were the two new trucks and the buffaloes and the six new unauthorized shops and so on. But all these, Phoolwati emphasized, were small change compared to the real money-spinner, which was people. Sundar was the only slum-lord who could mobilize a mob of several thousand people at less than a day's notice. This talent had won him the favours and gratitude of all the major political parties.

'You name them, he knows them!' Phoolwati said proudly, and reeled off the names of a dozen prominent political personages, all of whom, she boasted, were in Sundar's pocket.

Sundar's growing importance was brought home to me

by the smart salutes he received from the local policemen as he strutted about the neighbourhood surrounded by his henchmen. There was no doubt about it, Sundar was now a very important and powerful man, and my precious Phoolwati was his beloved wife.

THIRTY-TWO

I had all but dropped out of school. I spent my spare time hanging around the premises of the Shiv Mohan Band or idling at home while Phoolwati attended to her various enterprises. Finally, exasperated by my indolence, she insisted that I enroll in a cooking class. And so, three evenings a week, I found myself mastering the intricacies of Chinese, Western and Indian cuisines. Having never eaten anything more complicated than Phoolwati's famed stuffed parathas and the rather bland and insipid food that had prevailed at Roxanne's, I found the whole exercise an amazing waste of time and soon dropped out of the course.

Kalki was wooing me once again with something resembling his old ardour. Yet he had evidently not forgotten Sundar's drubbing and continued to maintain a degree of reserve in his courtship.

Kalki was in the habit of investing his entire salary, plus the considerable tips the bandwallahs extracted from the bridegrooms and their friends, on lottery tickets. He was certain that, one day, he would find himself a millionaire. He would urge me to ask the pandit for a 'system', a foolproof astrological methodology upon which he could base his 'investments', as he grandly called them.

He had, of course, no idea about the extent to which the pandit loathed him.

'Let's ask him to give us a system, Pooja,' he would plead. 'After all, he owes it to you. If your grandmother hadn't built this temple, where would he be today?'

Kalki had also taken to habitually 'borrowing' money from me. Since I had no income of my own, I had to resort to regularly pilfering small amounts of cash from the bundles of hundred rupee notes which Phoolwati stashed around the house in various improbable places, 'for safety', as she put it.

He also owed money to almost the entire number of the Shiv Mohan Band. These debts were always being rotated and rescheduled, awaiting the eventual windfall, about which the bandwallahs were as convinced as Kalki himself.

I personally found the lottery stalls revolting. Situated as they were next to the public urinals, these stalls were always crowded with hordes of dispirited, dissolute, unshaven men, some of them drunk, some drugged, all, it struck me, losers to the core. It hurt and disturbed me to see Kalki drawn there as though by a magnet, to see his handsome radiant face marred by a scowl, as he threw away the latest batch of dud tickets into the gutter and lit up a cheroot to mask his feelings. I wanted desperately to comfort him; I wished I were an heiress, so that I could shower him with all the good things he so richly deserved.

A nebulous plan was forming in my mind. I was not penniless. I possessed a gold coin of great value. I would retrieve the fortune Saboo had inadvertently dug up. I would be rich, and Kalki would be happy. It was as simple and clear as that.

I was not blind to the realities of Kalki's nature, nor had I forgotten the lessons of my mother, the inept prostitute, with her pitiable habit of falling in love. In spite of my total and consuming infatuation, I understood well that there was something both noble and base about Kalki. I refrained from telling him about the treasure. I would surprise him with it at the appropriate time. I would use the gold to buy him.

I decided to employ Phoolwati's help in recovering the gold. Without disclosing my immediate motives, I told her about the coin I had stolen from the oilcloth bag and the whole fantastic tale of Saboo's unwitting discovery of treasure while he was digging Shambhu's grave. Phoolwati wanted to know all the details: how Shambhu had looked in death, whether his bad eye had been open or closed, how much blood there had been and things like that. I could not satiate her morbid curiosity; she was more interested in the graphic details of Shambhu's murder than in my story about the gold.

'He got the death he deserved,' she said with relish. 'I only hope that it was not instantaneous. Someday I will repay that Saboo for the favour he did me. The poor man went to jail for his actions, while I got all this!' She looked around appreciatively at our opulent surroundings.

'I was telling you about the treasure,' I said. Phoolwati's lack of concentration was most irritating. Once she was on the gratifying subject of Shambhu's death, it was difficult to get her interested in anything else. But when I showed her the gold coin, her practical instincts came alive and she was all attention. She made me repeat the story not once but twice, once to her and then to Sundar, who was summoned from a conclave of his taporis and henchmen to hear the tale.

They examined the coin in wonder. The gold had a dull yellow sheen, and Sundar weighed it, clinked it, tapped it, juggled it about his hands and examined it in a hundred different ways before pronouncing that it was gold all right.

'It's not just the gold,' Phoolwati explained. 'These old things have a value which is quite different.'

They made me draw a map to explain exactly where Saboo had dug up the gold and the spot where grandmother had subsequently buried it. Phoolwati took the coin from me and locked it carefully in a secret cubbyhole in the safe of her steel cupboard, promising to have it assessed by a fence she knew who was knowledgeable about antiques.

When we next visited the temple we took a casual stroll around the buildings, which were as usual in a state of permanent construction, with girders and bags of cement strewn about the place. I pointed out the spot behind the peepul tree where grandmother had re-interred the gold coins. We went back to the temple and settled down for a chat with Pandit Kailash Shastry.

Grandmother's statue, resplendant in marble, gave me the creeps. I had begun to avoid visiting the temple after its installation. It was however a big hit with the public, and people from all walks of life thronged to the temple for grandmother's blessings.

Phoolwati started off with exquisite flattery about the pandit's talents. 'Don't you agree, Gudiya?' she would repeat after every hyperbolical illustration of Kailash Shastry's prophetic powers, concluding as usual with the oft-repeated story of the pandit's prognostication regarding her own second marriage 'to a strong and powerful man'.

Tactfully, she steered the subject around to the modification of the temple according to the precepts of the Vastu Shastra. This was a subject dear to the pandit's heart. The temple had come up in a haphazard and eclectic way. It followed none of the architectural or other guidelines prescribed by orthodox Hindu tradition for the purposes. A temple, the pandit explained, warming to the subject, was to be sited near a river or by a mountain. There were certain auspicious directions and others which had to be avoided at all costs. The main entrance, which in our temple faced south, should, according to him, have had a northern orientation. Then there was the question of the garbha griha and the mahamandapam, both of which were built without any regard for the appropriate proportions or auspicious directions.

Phoolwati agreed with everything he said, looking wise and knowing, as though she herself were a learned panditain.

'Last night I dreamt of Mataji,' she said earnestly. 'Gudiya's grandmother came to me in my dreams. She told me, "Phoolwati, I have a task for you. Get Sundar to build a shrine to Lord Shiva under the peepul tree. He has to do this personally, with his own hands. In this way he can atone for the wicked ways in which he earns his living." I told Sundar of my dream, Panditji, and he is of the same mind as me. We would like to undertake this holy task.'

While Phoolwati was reporting grandmother's

instructions her voice became wavery and garbled, as Ammi's had been. She was so convincing that I wondered why she had said nothing about it earlier, until it dawned on me that we could now access the gold coins without arousing suspicion. Panditji was all enthusiasm and promised the speedy onset of all kinds of heavenly blessings to Sundar and Phoolwati for undertaking God's work.

When we returned home, Phoolwati told Sundar about her plan. Sundar was, as always, full of effusive praise for his wife's ingenuity and wit. 'I tell you, Gudiya,' he said fondly, 'no one in the whole of India can match my Phoolwati for brains. M.A., B.A., Ph.D.—she is cleverer than all that. Look at this idea—it is a real two-in-one plan—we earn Lord Shiva's blessings for building the temple and we get our hands on the gold as well. If they made my Phoolwati the prime minister of India, she could solve all the problems of this country. I would like to give a reward of ten thousand rupees to that Saboo, wherever he is.'

THIRTY-THREE

Phoolwati was overcome with excitement at the prospect of unearthing the treasure. She did not want for money. More than the sheer financial considerations, it was a sense of adventure which drove her to frenzied and incessant planning on how to recover the gold.

Pandit Kailash Shastry had been dispatched to Hardwar on a fictitious mission. Sundar, assisted by one of his trusted taporis, was to perform the 'kar seva' and personally begin the construction of the Shiva shrine on an auspicious Monday morning.

We were by now the proud possessors of a telephone instrument. Sundar Pahalwan's connections had ensured that. One day I got a call from Sharp House. Roxanne had returned from an extended visit to America. She was aware that I had all but dropped out from school. She wanted very much to see me again, and would I please join her for dinner?

After the gaudy opulence of Phoolwati's kothi, Sharp House seemed understated and elegant. I was almost nostalgic about my brief stay there, and the entirely different life that would have been mine had I consented to being 'adopted' by Roxanne Lamba.

Roxanne was looking tired after the long flight. Her face was wan and there was a puffiness around her eyes I had never noticed before. Her mother, Mrs Dubash, was ill and had been admitted to hospital in Bombay. She asked me a few abstract questions about my absences from school. I responded with an inventive account of Phoolwati's continuing ill-health, which had supposedly kept me at home. In fact, I had totally abandoned the very idea of school and studies. I lied in good conscience, for Roxanne was so worried about her mother's health that I did not want to add to her worries.

We sat down for dinner at the oval dining table with clawed feet. Mr Lamba had materialized, accompanied by Roxanne's nephew, Cyrus. The son of Roxanne's deceased sister, Cyrus was devastatingly handsome, and completely oblivious to my presence. I could not help but compare him with Kalki, and discovered to my mortification that, in spite of his cocky good looks and his desperate desire to make good, Kalki appeared, in the balance, all said and done, a riff-raff footpath wallah.

Mr Lamba greeted me coldly and then proceeded to ignore me altogether. Roxanne was making anxious enquiries about doctors and nurses and hospital rooms, to which her nephew replied in a curious high-pitched voice. I decided that first impressions were deceptive and that Cyrus wasn't a patch on Kalki after all.

The two men got involved in a complicated argument about the exact implications of a new levy the government had enforced upon medium-level companies. Roxanne was toying absently with the first course, which was a freshwater rahu poached in a sickly looking greenish sauce. The fish was fresh, but, as usual, I found it a little insipid for my more rustic tastes. I was just reaching out for some salt when I realized that Roxanne was choking on her food and that her face had turned a strange shade of purple.

Mr Lamba and her nephew noticed her condition at the same time as I did. Cyrus rushed to the kitchen to get some bread, which he urged his aunt to swallow. Ma'am was clutching at her throat, making strangled sounds, low grunts which emanated not from her larynx but somewhere near her chest. Puzzlement and panic flooded her face. I knew that look; I had seen it before, in my Ammi's eyes.

Mr Lamba opened her mouth and tried to force a finger down her throat. He and Cyrus manouvered her to the sofa, where they lay her down. Roxanne attempted to sit up. There was an expression of appeal, of beseechment, in her eyes. She was speaking to herself. 'Asta vidat,' she said, her voice faltering. I thought she smiled, but I could not be sure. 'Ah, Deanna!' she murmured, and her eyes moved rapidly in their sockets. Then she grunted again, like a forlorn animal, and a loud emission of wind escaped her, followed by an overpowering stench.

I turned to her nephew in horror. He was staring at her pale-faced; fear and astonishment distorting his handsome face. We shook her and tried to rouse her, but she made no response.

Mr Lamba had already left to search for a doctor. The dogs were baying outside, as if they knew what had happened. The servants were huddled around the kitchen door, peering in anxiously through the little lobby near the staircase. They had sensed disaster and were whispering uneasily to each other.

Cyrus was on the telephone, trying to locate a doctor, an ambulance, anything. I stood beside Roxanne's body, praying for a miracle. I appealed to my Ammi to bring Ma'am back to life. Soon everything would be all right, Mr Lamba would arrive with a doctor, and they would give her an injection, put her on a drip and those myopic eyes would flutter to life again. I was sure it would be like that.

Mr Lamba was taking forever to return with the doctor. Cyrus had not been able to contact anybody on the phone. Now he was back with Roxanne. His already pale skin had turned a spectral white. I held his hands to reassure him. They were ice cold, but he did not reject the pressure of my touch. 'It's touch and go,' he said. 'I must rush to find a doctor.'

I was left alone with Roxanne. I examined her face, gentle and kind in repose. She was the only entirely good person I had ever encountered. From the time I had joined St. Jude's, she had encouraged me to believe in myself and to trust in myself, and she in turn had always trusted and believed in me. I had not repaid her faith; I had not managed to demonstrate my love.

The cuckoo clock on the wall, which had been out of order for as long as I could remember, suddenly opened its cheery red door. A ridiculous little bird came out and cuckooed twelve times. It would not stop; it went on and on. I had to stuff it under the pillow to gag it.

• symbolic of the loss of time

I looked at my watch. It was only eleven. The dogs were still howling outside. I was alone in the room with a corpse. A strong sense of the supernatural, a blank terror of death and the unknown spaces beyond, possessed me. I wanted to run away, to return to the temple, to sit safe in the warmth of Phoolwati's arms.

Death was no stranger to me. I had seen my Mamaji dangling from the mango tree in the courtyard and one-eyed Shambhu sprawled under the peepul tree. And then my grandmother, seated in her grotesque and unnatural samadhi. Now Roxanne Ma'am too had joined the other world. She had become a fravashi. The spirit had departed from her body. I could not imagine her rubbing shoulders with Magoo and Shambhu and the man with the laughing red mouth. It suddenly struck me that I had no real proof that I was alive; perhaps I too was dead. The dogs had not stopped baying. Everything else was still and silent. I pinched myself to check if it hurt.

Just then my Ammi's voice came forth to reassure me. The clock had probably been repaired in my absence, and not very well at that. Roxanne was dead and I was not, and there was nothing I could do about it.

Mr Lamba rushed in, looking distraught and dishevelled. He was accompanied by a man in a blue pashmina dressing gown. 'There she is, doctor!' he said, pushing him towards Roxanne.

Cyrus returned as well, with the family doctor in tow. For once, he was not laughing. They got busy with Roxanne, feeling her pulse, groping around with a stethoscope and putting little tubes up her nose. The unhurried way they went about it confirmed that it was only a formality. The doctor in the pashmina dressing gown made a clucking reproving sound and informed us that the patient was dead. Their family doctor fiddled about and closed her eyes. The left one remained half-open, and her gentle gaze followed me around the room.

The cook entered the room, staggering under a heavy tray laden with six cups of steaming coffee. When he saw Roxanne lying quite still on the sofa and realized what had happened, he dropped the tray with a dreadful clatter and ran sobbing out of the room.

Cyrus was busy on the telephone to Bombay. Mr Lamba was sitting with the two doctors, who were between them drafting out a death certificate. One of the servants was mopping up the coffee which the cook had dropped. Roxanne was lying on the sofa, her left eye impartially observing the chaos.

I wanted above all things to demonstrate my love, to bring some ritual and dignity to her departure. I ran upstairs to Roxanne's bedroom, oblivious to the ghosts that inhabited it, and rummaged through her drawers until I found the eagle feather she had once placed under my pillow, very long ago. I located the candles kept in reserve for power cuts. Returning to the living room, I gathered together three elaborately carved peg-tables and set up a sort of makeshift altar, with six candles arranged on cut-glass ashtrays. I knelt down. Placing the feather beneath her head, I ceremoniously kissed her damp forehead. Then I ran out of the room, out into the dark, all the way to Phoolwati's house.

THIRTY-FOUR

Panditji had returned within a day from Hardwar, quite upsetting Phoolwati's schedule. He appeared not at all surprised by Roxanne's demise and forbade me expressly from attending her funeral or any other associated ceremonies. He warned that a very unfortunate conjunction of planets was afoot. Under no circumstance was I to leave home for the next eight days. Phoolwati took his word as law and, despite my protests, put me under virtual house arrest for a week.

Phoolwati and Sundar Pahalwan went to the funeral, which was at the cemetery near Khan Market. She gave me a detailed account of the burial. There had been some wrangling over procedure, for by marrying a Hindu, if Mr Lamba could be called that, Roxanne had repudiated her Zoroastrian ancestry, and yet she was a practising Parsi. Phoolwati did not know exactly what had happened, but the funeral was very moving, with mountains of flowers which she described to me with professional interest and appreciation. There was a line of foreign cars and a full turnout of Delhi's rich and powerful, Phoolwati reported with satisfaction.

Roxanne had told me about the Towers of Silence in Bombay where the bodies of devout Parsis were returned to the elements, to be devoured by vultures. I told Phoolwati about it, for she had usually a taste for the morbid. Her eyes crinkled up with disbelief, and she told me righteously not to joke about the dead.

Phoolwati's appetite for the dramatic had been whetted by Roxanne's sudden departure from this world. She talked about it incessantly, with a undisguised self-satisfaction in outliving her rival for my affections. 'It was the food they ate,' she said, 'all English-style nonsense. If you eat with your fingers you can feel a fish-bone before it gets stuck in your throat, but this fork and knife always kills people! After all there is some sense in our ancient Indian ways.'

Soon the nine-day wonder of Roxanne's death had passed. Phoolwati was worrying about how to deal with the pandit's presence in the temple while digging for the gold. Fate provided a fortuitous way out by striking him down with a virulent cold. Phoolwati visited him, armed with her bottle of Phenargan cough syrup, and persuaded him to consume the entire bottle, insisting that the doctor had prescribed just that when she was down with the flu.

After Pandit Kailash Shastry had fallen into an inescapable opiate slumber, and a crescent moon hung suspended over the peepul tree, Phoolwati and Sundar got down to the job of digging. That is to say, Sundar dug, and Phoolwati and I directed him. He was a powerfully built man; mud and brick and concrete yielded to him like putty.

Phoolwati was to keep an eye out for the gold, and she kept urging him not to dig so vigorously, for he might split the oilskin bag and scatter the treasure. It was my job to look out for any interlopers.

Sundar and I had already been briefed about another convenient 'dream' wherein grandmother had instructed Phoolwati and Sundar to start digging straight away. I was quite sceptical about the need for such elaborate alibis, but Phoolwati was a great one for contingency plans and fallbacks. I had not visited the peepul tree for a very long time. The swish of its large beautifully shaped leaves still carried the suggestion of a million slumbering presences. I knew they were all safe in its branches, the ghouls and familiars and forgotten friends of my childhood, silenced for the moment, perhaps, before Phoolwati's overpractical presence, waiting only for the slightest indication from me to make themselves once again manifest.

Phoolwati was a devout believer in Lord Shiva. He stood way ahead of Lord Krishna or Lord Rama or Hanuman in her pantheon. She had awarded him the ultimate accolade— he was, according to her, 'A Real Man'. Now, she was singing a hymn to Lord Shiva in a soft Bhojpuri dialect, directing meaningful and amorous glances at Sundar as she sang. He was not deflected from his task, and continued digging up brick and stone with single-minded determination.

Suddenly I felt an electric shiver in my spine, and the fine brown hairs on my arms stood up on end, alerted and afraid. I looked around in terror, and, there, high on the branches of my peepul tree, was one-eyed Shambhu, his face lit up by the petro-max in Phoolwati's hands, staring at Sundar and Phoolwati with extreme ire. I screamed out in terror, but Phoolwati hushed me and told me to be quiet, or I would wake the pandit up.

Shambhu seemed to have noticed me and flashed me the well-remembered smile, the normal, reassuring smile he used to give me when he presented me an extra biscuit with my tea.

At that very moment, Sundar struck gold. I heard the sound of metal striking metal and looked around involuntarily for my Ammi's comforting presence. But this was now, and here was Phoolwati doing an excited war dance, leaping nimbly about, carrying her enormous body with her in unexpected grace. A shower of gold mohurs lay at our feet, magical, golden, shining with assurance and permanence. I was speechless with emotion, and tears stung my eyes. I did not care for the gold at all; I was weeping for my grandmother.

Phoolwati scooped up the gold in the pallav of her sari, exposing her unbelievable bosom as she did so. The coins made a clinking sound, then rolled about and fell this way and that. They could not be contained in the flimsy cloth of her sari. She gathered them up again, then retrieved the two that had rolled into the deep cleavage of her enormous mammaries. She slipped the coins back into the oilskin bag, carefully counting them as she went along. Tearing a strip of cloth from her sari pallav, she tied it around the oilskin bag. She handed the package to me and began checking the debris of dug-up mud and concrete, crawling about on all fours to make sure that no gold was left behind. Then she signalled us to leave.

But Sundar Pahalwan would not stop digging. He seemed possessed by some diabolic source of energy. His shovel struck at the earth with manic strength, on and on and on. A strong wind was rising, and little flurries of mud and dirt rose around him, like ghostly attendants. Phoolwati shouted at him to stop, quite forgetting her own earlier admonitions about stealth and silence. Still he continued digging.

'There must be more of it; there may be more gold coins around,' he said distractedly, still digging with that unnerving vigor.

The peepul tree rustled and murmured in the wind. I looked up to see if it was Shambhu, but there was nobody. I snapped my fingers before my mouth, just to be sure, and urged Phoolwati to get going. She waddled over to Sundar, took the shovel from him and, holding him by the shoulders, firmly steered him homewards.

Sundar showed the gold to his 'contact' the very next day. First he took a single gold coin to have it assessed. Then, armed with a pistol, and accompanied by two trusted taporis, he took the entire treasure. He returned looking extremely satisfied, carrying three briefcases stacked with currency notes.

'Our Gudiya is a very rich girl now,' he said. 'The girl is an incarnation of Lakshmi. Her husband will be a lucky man!'

She relieved him of the suitcase and stashed it into a steel cupboard. Then, after locking it securely, she gave me the key. 'One key for you and one for me,' she said, 'but the money is yours; never forget it.'

Sundar told me that the coins were from the time of Emperor Jehangir and carried the impress of his portrait and the profile of his beloved Empress Noorjehan. His 'contact' was an authority on antiques and numismatics, and he assured me that we had got the best possible price under the circumstances.

'If the government came to know about it, the bastards would take it all and lock it up in a museum,' he said self-righteously. 'I had to move it out fast.'

The stacks of notes seemed enough to keep me in comfort forever. I told Phoolwati to take some of the money, for it was after all she and Sundar Pahalwan who had retrieved it, but she indignantly spurned the offer.

The Shiva temple was no nearer getting built, and Pandit Kailash Shastry was getting restless. Sundar had dug up the area around the peepul tree with mindless abandon. It was strewn with debris, and now neither he nor Phoolwati was in any hurry to carry on with the construction.

Panditji kept urging Phoolwati to complete the task she had so eagerly undertaken, but she took refuge in yet another convenient 'dream' wherein grandmother urged her to be cautious and cease all building activity until further sanction, which was to be granted through another vision.

Kailash Shastry decided to resort to a miracle of his own. A cracked and ancient looking statue of Lord Shiva spontaneously materialized near the peepul tree, amidst the mad mess Sundar had created while digging up the gold.

The miracle was duly proclaimed to the faithful. In no time at all, well-heeled devotees were scrambling for the prerogative of constructing the Shiva shrine. Phoolwati, always astute to the ebbs and flows of public opinion, duly pulled rank. Grandmother promptly appeared in a dream and announced that, as the statue had now been found, Sundar and Phoolwati could proceed with their divinely allocated task.

A few weeks later, Roxanne's driver, Bhimsingh, arrived in Phoolwati's house with a typed letter. It was from a firm of lawyers, with their offices in Connaught Place, requesting me to meet them in their chambers at 10 a.m. the next day, subject to confirmation.

Phoolwati promptly appropriated the letter and took it to Pandit Kailash Shastry for his astrological judgement. He consulted his almanac intently before replying.

'The letter is an important one, and the sender means well. However, as it was delivered at an inauspicious time, during the dominance of Rahu-kalam, much could come of it, or nothing. I cannot say any more.'

Phoolwati urged him to commit himself further, to say something specific, but he would not be moved beyond those sphinx-like utterances.

Phoolwati insisted on accompanying me to the lawyers' offices. She wore a South Indian silk sari and a pair of expensive dark glasses, and when we alighted from our taxi outside the office building we looked as well born and well bred a duo as any.

A timid looking clerk escorted us up. Mr Lamba and Cyrus were waiting in the chambers. We settled down on the plush leather sofas. The table between us was laden with files and law books. Mr Lamba was the first to speak. 'We are here to discuss the terms of my wife Roxanne's will,' he said in English waving his arms about agitatedly. 'I am eager to make a fair and speedy settlement. I wish Pooja nothing but the best.' I wasn't listening; I was distracted by the sight of Roxanne's husband. I had never before noticed how hairy his arms were.

'Are you listening, Gudiya?' he asked sternly. I wanted to tell him that I was Pooja, not Gudiya, but decided not to. He repeated what he had said before, in a slow, careful voice.

Phoolwati pretended to have understood, but I translated what he had said into Hindi for her benefit anyway.

Cyrus was examining me with bemused interest, as though I were a hitherto innocuous species of insect which was suddenly displaying aberrational behaviour.

The lawyer told Mr Lamba to keep silent; it was not in his interest to speak. Then he cleared his throat and explained the terms of Roxanne's will to us.

The bulk of Roxanne's fortune was to be evenly divided between her husband, Mr Lamba, and her nephew, Cyrus Batliboy. However there was a not insubstantial portion of trust funds, in the form of stocks and securities, which Roxanne stood to inherit from her mother, Mrs Dubash. These she had endowed in equal part to me and the St. Jude's Academy for the Socially Handicapped.

Thereafter, continued the lawyer, stopping for a long breath, Roxanne's mother, who was currently in the Breach Candy Hospital undergoing treatment, had decided to revoke her own will in view of the terms of Roxanne's bequest. Mr Lamba and Mr Cyrus Batliboy were to be the new beneficiaries.

'But I thought Mrs Dubash is too ill to understand anything! She has been in a coma for months,' I interjected.

Mr Lamba and Cyrus exchanged looks. The lawyer gave me a soothing smile. 'Not at all, Miss, er, Pooja,' he said smoothly. 'She is in full possession of all her faculties. We are quite assured of that.'

Something was not right. 'Mummy' had approved of me; she was even fond of me. Mrs Dubash was always inclined to charity and very proud of the good work Roxanne was doing at St. Jude's. In any case, her hatred of her upstart son-in-law far exceeded her feelings for me or St. Jude's.

The lawyer was not through. Both Mr Lamba and Cyrus were inclined to honour the sentiments of Roxanne's will, and, if I were to sign a waiver, they would ensure that I was given a sufficient sum of money, out of their own pockets, if necessary.

'What about St. Jude's?' I asked. 'How will you deal with them?'

I was informed that my query had no bearing on the matter at hand and in any case the St. Jude's Academy for the Socially Handicapped was not an individual but a trust.

I conferred with Phoolwati, after explaining the situation to her in Hindi. The lawyer interrupted us to stress that were I to take a contrary view, I would almost certainly be a loser, for I would gain nothing and be put to needless out-of-pocket expense.

I looked at Cyrus with his handsome face and his well-cut suit and then at Mr Lamba with his shock of grey hair. I remembered Roxanne's gentle face and myopic eyes and I took an instant and irrevocable decision.

'I don't want it,' I said. 'I won't take anything from the two of you. Yet if Roxanne left me any money, if she believed in me, if it is my due, I will not refuse it. Let me talk to the teachers in St. Jude's before I decide that.'

Phoolwati gave me a concerned look. Mr Lamba looked indignant. Cyrus was as polite and distant as ever.

The lawyer shuffled his papers. 'Very well,' he said. 'We shall continue to keep in touch with you. If you decide to change your mind, my clients are keen to honour, at least in token, the sentiments of Mrs Lamba's will.'

'Thank you,' I said politely. 'I shall let you know of my decision.' Mustering all the dignity due to Pooja Abhimanyu Singh, I swept out of the room, with Phoolwati following meekly in my wake.

THIRTY-FIVE

I was rich, young and beautiful and perhaps potentially even a heiress. Some innate wisdom had restrained me from telling Kalki about the gold, but I suspected that he was aware of the conditions of Roxanne's will. Perhaps this had excited his affections, for he was beginning to talk about marriage with an increasing degree of impatience.

I discovered that I was four months pregnant. The bouts of morning sickness and the delayed periods were confirmed as 'good news' by the lady doctor after a laboratory test. Phoolwati and I had taken a sample of my early morning urine to the doctor's clinic in a rickety autorickshaw, in the course of which a small quantity of the substance had spilt on to my clothes.

Phoolwati's first reaction was to swear me to absolute secrecy about my condition. 'Sundar will kill both of you if he finds out,' she said, her face ashen. I had never before seen Phoolwati afraid, and the sight unnerved me. After we paid the fees to the incredibly sophisticated receptionist, we returned home, frightened and confused.

I no longer wanted to marry Kalki. The only other option was an abortion. Phoolwati, who had hungered for a child all her life, recoiled from the idea.

'What kind of daayan would contemplate killing her own child?' she asked in horror, when I tentatively suggested the alternative. 'No Gudiya, you can't do that.'

We consulted another lady doctor and were told that an abortion was no longer possible, as the pregnancy had progressed too far. 'If you had come to me a month earlier,' she said, her spectacles glinting in the cold fluorescent light, 'it would have been another matter altogether.'

We were married within a week. It should have been the happiest day of my life. The entire temple premises were bedecked with swaying toranas of tender green mango leaves. All ordinary devotees and outsiders were turned away by a sign which announced that the temple was closed to the public because of a 'Family Function'. Phoolwati personally supervised the mali who set up the wedding mandapam. It was pillared with four young banana stems the colour of ivory, and the most wondrous flowers, the likes of which I had never seen, were strung through it like jewels.

Phoolwati was, as usual, full of surprises, and she unlocked yet another of her ever-expanding fleet of steel cupboards to display a carefully put-together trousseau, consisting of twenty-one silk saris and eleven sets of jewellery. 'Your Ammi had told me to keep these ready,' she said matter-of-factly, before setting about to organize things with lightning speed.

We got married in the mid-afternoon. Pandit Kailash Shastry, resplendent in a yellow silk dhoti, had chosen the exact time and muhurtam with infinite care and precision. We were to exchange garlands at forty-six minutes past three on the dot, and an alarm clock had been kept aside for the specific purpose of alerting us to the advent of the auspicious time.

The pandit called Kalki and me aside for a private chat. There were, according to the shastras, eight forms of marriage, he explained. These were the Brahma, the Daiva, the Prajapatya, the Arsa, the Gandharva, the Asura, the Paisacha and Rakshasa. Of these, the Gandharva vivah, the choosing of a partner between two individuals for the consideration of love, was the most precious to Kama deva, the God of Love.

'Gandharva vivah is an old-fashioned Sanskrit word which means "love marriage",' he explained, making a brave attempt at modernity. 'It is not selfish, unlike the Asura, the Paisacha and the Rakshasa, which are all demoniac, fiendish forms of marriage.' Kalki flicked back his hair and looked mutinous. Although he had been pushing me for an early marriage, he suddenly appeared reluctant, and even rebellious. A faint, stale smell of liquor sat on his breath, and his eyes were glazed over.

Contrary to Pandit Kailash Shastry and Phoolwati's specific instructions, he had come dressed in a suit, the same suit he had worn for Phoolwati's wedding. Sundar Pahalwan was about to rough him up to persuade him to change into a dhoti, but Phoolwati restrained him. 'What does it matter?' she said philosophically. 'You can't change what's inside the dhoti!'

Sundar and Phoolwati were to perform the kanyadaan

and give me away. I was wearing a yellow and gold sari, one of Phoolwati's twenty-one, and a hastily assembled blouse which Phoolwati had herself sat up stitching late into the night. I looked into the mirror and knew that I was beautiful. Yet there was something not quite right. I had the nagging unease of something unremembered and undone.

'Where's my trunk?' I asked Phoolwati. Ignoring the pandit's concerned looks and Kalki's irritation, I took Phoolwati by the arm and ran all the way to her house. Oblivious of the dust settling on my hair and sari, I balanced on a stool and retrieved my oldest possession from the top of yet another of Phoolwati's steel cupboards. A well-remembered smell of musk and mothballs rose from it, and I started weeping uncontrollably, sweet, comforting tears of nostalgia and hope.

Phoolwati stroked my hair comfortingly. 'All girls cry on their wedding day,' she said. 'It's a law of nature. As for Kalki, don't get upset if he sulks and acts difficult. Remember, you're both young; it'll take time to adjust.'

But that was not what I was weeping about. I was busy rummaging through the old clothes. They were, to my adult eyes, pathetically shorn of their remembered glamour and mystery. I found the odhni I had been searching for. It was a green georgette chunni with a glorious orange border of embroidered gold ambis. I settled the chunni around my shoulders, wiped the tears from my eyes and told Phoolwati that I was ready to return. 'Not like that,' she said gently, and covered my head with the odhni, in an elaborately modest ghunghat.

I had not invited anybody to attend our nuptials. Kalki

had come accompanied by the entire contingent of the Shiv Mohan Band. Punctually at three forty-six in the afternoon, when the auspicious moment arrived, they struck up a merry tune. We exchanged garlands and took the seven steps around the sacred fire. After it was all over, when the pandit was untying the knot which bound Kalki's angavastram, hastily improvised from a scarf, to my odhini, Phoolwati announced that she would sing a 'Mangalashtak', allegedly of her own composition.

It was a plaintive and pretty song in which she invoked, successively, Lord Vishnu and his consort Lakshmi; Brahma and Sarasvati; Shiva and Parvati; the Sun and his wife Chhaya; the Moon and his wife Rohini; Indra and Sati; Vashishta and Arundhati; Rama and Sita; Krishna and Rukmini and several other pairs of gods and goddesses.

She had written down the words on a piece of paper, and, although Sundar and the pandit looked most appreciative, I thought she went on interminably. Kalki scowled and said that he wanted to smoke a beedi, and I myself was itching to use the toilet. At last the song concluded, and Phoolwati mollified Kalki somewhat by presenting him with a gold and diamond ring and an expensive looking wristwatch.

Sundar Pahalwan led the bridegroom's party to the tent which had been put up outside the temple gates, where Phoolwati had contracted with the halvai from the local sweetshop to prepare samosas and cholas and all sorts of sweetmeats, ordered on her usual extravagant scale. As the bandwallahs began tucking into their food, Pandit Kailash Shastry cornered Kalki and me.

'There is something I have been wanting to ask you, young man,' he said sweetly. 'In spite of the extraordinary circumstances of your marriage, it is my duty to ask you this. What is your gotra, young man?' Kalki looked blank.

'Ah, so you don't know,' the pandit continued triumphantly. 'I thought as much. Anyway, I think I am entitled to ask you what your surname is. Who was or is your father?'

'My surname is Thakur,' Kalki replied arrogantly.

'Thakur,' I said to myself.

'Thakur!' the pandit repeated after me. 'Everybody can claim to be a Thakur in this Kalyug! However, I want to point out to you, Mr Thakur, that there are certain aspects of your horoscope which I confess have been troubling me. At the moment, Venus and Mars are conjoining the seventh house. Otherwise also, there are other things, which I would rather not spell out just now . . .'

'So what should I do?' Kalki snarled. His fine lips were distorted with anger. I wondered detachedly what I had ever seen in him.

The pandit seized the advantage at once. 'But there is nothing to worry,' he said grandly, with the air of someone producing a rabbit from a hat. 'Our Gudiya has been enjoying a gaja-kesari yoga for the last three years now—and it continues for the next seventeen years. Seventeen years of uninterrupted wealth, power, and success! You are a very lucky man! I think our Gudiya's stars will counterweigh any imbalances in your horoscope. Hari Om, Hari Om.' And he went into one of his famous trances, with his eyes closed and his face set in an inscrutable smile.

Phoolwati chose the moment to improvise a new twist to our already improbable marriage. 'Now we must all seek the blessing of our revered Mataji,' she said, and herded all of us, including the bemused bandwallahs, to the sanctum sanctorum where the statue of my grandmother presided over the marbled prayer hall.

'Kalki, Gudiya, touch your grandmother's feet and seek her blessings,' she said in a shrill, excited voice, her bosom heaving with accumulated emotion.

The bandwallahs examined the marbled likeness of my grandmother with a respectful curiosity. It could have been a moment of high farce, but fortunately they were well indoctrinated in religiosity, and the dozen of them unquestioningly fell to their feet. I bent down as well, and then looked up to examine my grandmother square in the face. Her marbled eyes were closed in contemplation, but the faintest smile, sceptical yet satisfied, played about her lips. Mr Shiv Mohan insisted that we return home with him. I realized that I was now Pooja Thakur. I said the name out aloud, to the surprise of myself and those around me.

THIRTY-SIX

M̲r Shiv Mohan, eponymous with the band, had provided us with accommodation in his own house. He had a large, noisy family. The room he put at our disposal was squalid and ill-ventilated. Phoolwati was already prospecting for better lodgings and informed me firmly that my child would be born and brought up in a style worthy of my 'background'.

So many years of changes and surprises had made me very adaptable, and I fell into the rhythm of my new life with a flexible ease. I spent most of the day, and the evenings when the band was commissioned to play at a wedding, with Phoolwati. Occasionally I would cook a light meal for Kalki. He was cool with me sexually and for the most part ignored me altogether. Sometimes, inexplicably, his lust would be aroused, and he would devour me with an animal passion that took me unawares. I had developed a voracious appetite for sex, and, although my girlish infatuation for Kalki had long since subsided, he could arouse another woman inside me who I never knew had existed.

I made regular visits to the gynaecologist, accompanied always by Phoolwati. I was in excellent physical health, but life with Kalki was taking its toll, and I found I was constantly tired and depressed. Kalki's ultimately coarse nature, his vanity and cruelty, wore me down to the extent that my considerable natural resilience seemed to have disappeared altogether.

Phoolwati constantly urged me to return to her house, but some vestigial shards of pride kept me away.

'The child will have a legitimate father now. Your Kalki has served his function. You can't waste your life like this, Gudiya, with these bandwallahs!' she exhorted.

The bandwallahs were surprisingly kind and affectionate, like a sort of extended family, supportive and understanding. I had resolved not to dip into my personal funds, or even to let Kalki know that they existed. Sometimes, when for weeks on end I received no housekeeping money from my impecunious husband, Kedar, the clarinet player, or even Mr Shiv Mohan himself would forward me a small bridging loan. Unasked, they would buy me groceries and give me occasional gifts of fruits or a box of sweetmeats brought back from some exceptionally extravagant wedding.

And yet there was never anything indiscreet or forward in their behaviour. They would always address me as Bhabhi and constantly showed me all the deference and respect due to a brother's wife.

Having heard of Ammi's legendary musical talents, Mr Shiv Mohan asked if I would consider becoming the lead singer for a party-band he was trying to organize.

'You know, disco-shisco,' he said, 'and a little dancing and hip-shaking with the troupe.'

Kalki too was very enthused by the idea. 'Why don't you agree, Pooja!' he said excitedly. 'Later we could even branch off on our own!'

I had to confess that I had been bequeathed with none of my grandmother's multifarious talents. I seemed instead to have inherited only my mother's propensity to get into trouble and unfortunate situations.

On the whole, I managed to maintain a brave front, and Phoolwati glimpsed very little of the agony I was undergoing. I was determinedly cheerful, but, inside, there was a deep, unutterable fear that this was how my whole life might pass—in indifference, indignities and calculated cruelties.

One night Kalki came home drunk and beat me up. The next day my body was bruised and my limbs ached, but my spirit, by some inexplicable alchemy of nature, was restored. I resolved to find a way out of the intolerable situation.

Shame and pride had kept me away from the temple, but that day I went back. Pandit Kailash Shastry was away on some business. Phoolwati too was not in her stall, which had been left in the charge of some Bhojpuri assistant. The temple compound was deserted. I listened to the rustling conversation of the peepul leaves and then summoned up the courage to confront the statue of my grandmother.

'Why!' I asked her. 'Why, why, why?'

Her marbled face looked almost tender, and as I stared deep into the knowing stone eyes I caught the shadow of an inscrutable grimace—a knowing, compounded of pain and ruthless courage.

Just then there was a little commotion. An autorickshaw driver who had halted outside the temple was having an altercation with a passenger. The old lady who was arguing about the fare looked so much like Ammi that I thought my mind was playing tricks with me. Shuddering with a delicious sense of anticipation, I rushed forth to greet her.

But it was only Lila returned from her pilgrimage. She sighed with wonder and joy at the sight of my extruding belly. As I felt her knobbly fingers and tough old wrists kneading my shoulders in embrace, strength and renewal flowed through my body like a rising sap. I felt invulnerable and unafraid, and I laughed at myself for my fears and uncertainties.

Lila was full of tales about the places and people she had encountered in the course of her pilgrimage. She had been to Dwarka, Kashi, Hardwar, Badrinath and then on to Pashupati. She had brought back innumerable packets of prasad, as well as a rudraksha rosary for Pandit Kailash Shastry, a shawl for Phoolwati and an amber necklace for me.

Her journey seemed to have given her a radical degree of confidence. I wondered maliciously how Phoolwati would cope with Lila's new avataar.

'How is your family, Lila?' I asked.

Lila looked pious. 'It's all God's maya, Gudiya Rani!' she replied, playing with her prayer beads as she spoke. 'When my children saw me throw all my gold ornaments, all twenty-two carat, mind you, into your grandmother's grave, somehow they lost interest in me. You could say that I'm a free woman now.'

I returned to our lodgings considerably uplifted. Lila's conversation had set off a new train of thought. The germ of an idea was formulating in my mind.

I was studiedly nice to Kalki after that. I was polite and painstakingly pleasant, and praised him constantly. I extolled his good looks, his musical talents and his loving temperament. 'Why don't you try your luck in Bombay again, Kalki?' I said disingenuously. 'I'm sure you could hit it big! You could get a break in films or even become a pop star!'

As I spoke, his handsome face lit up. He looked inhumanly, supremely beautiful, and I knew, suddenly, that it was not just a ploy. Kalki could, would, become all these things, and more.

His face fell again, and his features recomposed themselves into their familiar scowl. 'But I don't have the funds,' he said petulantly, 'you know I don't.'

I took off the thick gold necklace Phoolwati had gifted me, the earrings and the four gold bangles, and thrust them all at him. 'I'll get you the money, Kalki.' I said calmly. 'I'll sell my stridhan for you.'

And that was what I did. I went to the neighbourhood jeweller, and, swearing him to secrecy, disposed of my gold. Kalki and I went together to the railway station, where, after paying a bribe to the clerk, we purchased a single one-way ticket to Bombay, second-class sleeper. I ironed his shirts and his best and only suit. We bought him a pair of shiny new shoes, for the last pair was also worn out with all the ceaseless tramping through the dusty streets of Delhi as he played the trombone.

Kalki looked uncertainly at his uniform—the gold-braided red suit in which I had first encountered him and given him my heart. 'Should I take this?' he asked uncertainly. 'What do you think, Pooja?'

'Perhaps you should,' I replied, and we stuffed it somehow into the battered suitcase Kalki had purloined from a friend in the band.

Kalki was hungry, which was unusual. I made him a paratha, a stuffed paratha with onions and potatoes in it. As I cooked the paratha on the griddle, as it sizzled merrily in the little pool of desi ghee in which it was frying, my fingers touched the iron surface while turning it over. I burnt my finger, and later, when Kalki was about to leave, it was still hurting, reminding me that pain was a general principle of life.

I went with him to the railway station. The crowds, the excitement, the rushing porters and the garbled announcements transported me to another time. I was back in the ladies room in Bhusawal and then all those frenetic panicky days of relentless travel, before Riyasuddin Rizvi had deposited us on a lonely stretch of road, beneath the peepul tree.

The platform was awash with the smell of urine and disinfectant, each claiming ascendancy over the bustle of arriving and departing passengers. I loved the railway station; it was alive with change and transformation. From here one could go anywhere, one could do anything. And the children! There were brigades of them: dirty, unwashed children darting from train to train, platform to platform, building up mountains of debris and refuse in the platform. I saw the children cluster around a fat old trader and cut his pocket with careless glee. I saw a beggar with no hands or feet smoking a cigarette. I saw the look of disdain on his face as he heard the clink of coins on the board on which he perched. I saw all this and more while Kalki sat still and motionless on the iron bench beside me, for we had come early to the station and the train was, not unexpectedly, running late.

I savored the sounds and the names of the trains. The Bhopal Express, the Jammu Tavi. The Rajdhani Superfast. Here was romance and movement, in these trains, these names, these magical places, these destinations. This was a place where one could forget one's past and forge into one's future. I felt a rush of optimism. Things would be good for us, for Kalki and for me. I bought him a soft drink and one for me, an orange-flavored drink in a chilled bottle that hurt my finger where I had burnt it on the griddle.

The train lumbered in, air-conditioned cool escaping from its innards as the Delhi passengers tumbled out. The coolies in their white turbans and red kurtas crowded around the entrances to the vestibules. Kalki was tense and taciturn. He forgot his bag as he made his way into the train or perhaps he just knew I would carry it for him. He looked very young and unsure, even frightened. 'Why don't you come with me, Pooja?' he asked. 'We could seek our fortune together.'

'I'll be all right here,' I replied. 'Besides, there is the baby to think of.' A provocatively pretty girl was seated next to Kalki. She shot him an interested glance, but Kalki was, as usual, too preoccupied with his own thoughts. I felt a sharp stab of jealousy. The emotion surprised me. Did I still love him in the old mad way? I wondered with a tinge of panic. Then his face behind the shutters, and the sharp long whistle of the train, the sudden rush to the platform, which nearly knocked me down, and I was alone.

I did not return to the room in Shiv Mohan's house, but went straight in an autorickshaw to Phoolwati's kothi. Phoolwati was overjoyed to see me. Sensing at once that something had happened, she tactfully refrained from asking me any questions and instead launched into a chatty, distracted monologue about life in the temple.

'That half-witted Lila is back,' she said, 'full of big talk about Banares and Badrinath. Huh!' With that expressive dismissal, she moved on to her personal life. Sunder was on to 'a really big deal' in which a lot of 'high-ups' were involved. It was all 'top-class', although she didn't know precisely what was at stake as Sundar was being very secretive about it. Her talk soothed and settled me and made me forget about Kalki for a while.

THIRTY-SEVEN

The texture of my life changed after Kalki left. At first, I missed him physically. There was an aching sense of absence, and all the everyday acts of familiarity, the intimacy of two people who share a life, announced his departure. However, I was used to change—it had been a constant in my life. Except for my Ammi, who, in spite of her many surprising manifestations and avataars, continued to remain my Ammi, everything around me had retained a sort of recurring flux. So I accepted Kalki's departure with resignation, and even a degree of relief.

Who was he? Who had he been, this man I had so rashly given myself to? There were so many things about Kalki I did not know anything of. Yet I never wondered overmuch about where he was now. That was a question I avoided, for it brought a train of other questions with it.

I used to wonder about Kalki after he had left us. I was married and yet not married; Kalki was most certainly there, somewhere, but he was no longer here, at home, to trouble and torment me, with the authority that our marriage conferred.

Kalki was gone, but I could still not admit, not even to myself, that I was glad to be alone again. My mother had never had a husband. Neither, as far as I knew, had my grandmother. I had never known a father. There had been no models of masculinity to teach me the lessons of dependence as a woman. Even my Mamaji, who I imagined I remembered as a kindly and elegant figure in a well-cut sherwani, had honourably left the scene of the battle, hanging himself as he did from the mango tree in the courtyard. And yet I had acceded immediately and inevitably to the conditionings of womanhood, to some imagined scenario or script I might have picked up in a cinema hall, in the glycerine tears of a weeping heroine or a devasted second-lead younger sister. Why had I been so afraid of Kalki? Why had I let him beat and abuse me as I had done?

One answer, of course, was that he had been handsome beyond belief. I was already beginning to forget how exactly he had looked. Sometimes I could remember the cut of his face but not the exact colour of his eyes. Then, in memory again, his smile would appear before me, his mocking, victorious smile, and I would tremble with remembered love, my insides leaping with the memory of sexual desire, my lips aching for the touch of his. The tricks of memory mingled with those of desire, and perhaps these longing were sweet precisely because Kalki was not there to harass me in person.

I missed him, but I sensed in his absence an opportunity for growth, for escape, which I was determined not to miss. I loved Kalki, but love is not life, and the imperatives of survival pulled elsewhere. Every day, gradually and imperceptibly, his hold on me lessened. One day I found a photograph of his, taken after a wedding. He was surrounded by his friends, all in their shining red and gold uniforms. His was unbuttoned at the neck. He was flushed with laughter and the arrogance of his own beauty and a few shots of rum. Kalki looked so handsome that my heart leapt up in rapture, and then, suddenly, I was devastated by an extreme sense of loss. I looked at the photograph for a very long time, taking him in bit by bit: his heroic shoulders, the long straight lines of his neck and those lips that curved like an archer's bows. I looked deep into his eyes, but they didn't look back into mine; they were leery and furtive; he was laughing at a joke with his friends.

I rarely dream. I had a vivid dream about my childhood, the first I ever carried into my waking hours. I dreamt I was a baby again, in a room with soft lights and chandeliers. I was in the arms of a very tall man. I could not see his face, but the arms that held me were clothed in cream-colored embroidered brocade that felt soft and cool to the touch. I can still remember the feel of the soft embroidery against my plump baby cheeks. The man smiles, and I feel reassured by the flash of his teeth above the cream achhkan and his dark beard.

There is a piano playing in the background. In my dream, it is not a harmonium (as it must surely have been), but a piano, playing a pretty, tinkly tune I know and recognize. My baby body is still and secure in this man's arms, in this room with soft lights and chandeliers. I am content to simply wiggle my toes or clench and unclench my fingers.

And then there is a feeling of damp; my bottom is wet, as are my toes. The man is angry, I can see the flash of his white teeth, but he is no longer smiling. He is shouting and swearing and he throws me on the floor, or so I think, but I land on a soft pillow. I land with a thud on the pillow, the nape of my neck registers the fall and I whimper for a few seconds before I break into a loud wail. The man is shouting, I can no longer hear the tinkle of the piano and the lights from the chandelier are no longer soft—they glitter harshly in my tear-filled eyes. The woman comes towards me, her expression is reproachful but restrained as she picks me up and holds me to her bosom. She smells of roses and lemons and patchouli, and I know that this is Roxanne who is holding me, although she is dressed in unfamiliar clothes I cannot completely describe. I am uncertain whether I should be still or continue crying. The man has lapsed from anger into indifference, but he is still sulking. I can see his face now, and I recognize it. It is Kalki.

The dream would not leave me, it followed me around and it clung to me like a damp odour through the waking day. For weeks this dream persisted in staying with me, though I tried to shake it off with all sorts of useful activity. I pickled a jar of red peppers. I had bought them from a street vendor I knew. He gave them to me cheap and ensured me of their bite and pungency. I was enchanted by their colour, by the purity of the bright splash of red in the plastic bag, by their size and shape and strength. I washed them carefully and dried them in the sun, and then I slit them from neck to tip with careful, precise movements. I had prepared the stuffing already, with lemon and cumin and aniseed and turmeric, roasted and ground and judiciously balanced with just a hint of jaggery and asofetida.

I put them in a jar I appropriated from the tea shop, and they smiled at me affectionately from behind the glass walls of their new prison. I left the jar in the sun to settle, to seep in the sharp smells of lemon and vinegar and mustard oil. My hair was in my eyes, it had escaped from the perfunctory bun into which I had tied it and as I flicked it back I felt the oil and chilli sting my eyes and I wept with pain again. The smell of mustard and chilli clung to me all night, as I tossed and turned in my pillow, unable to sleep, unable to dream.

Every morning I would put the pickled chillies out in the sun, and every evening I would bring them in again. I would lift up the lid and savour the sharp high smell that rose from the bottle. In the evening as the sun set I would take the bottle in. As the days passed the flavours settled in and the red of the chilli peppers mellowed to a duller shade.

I was determined not to hurry, to let the pickle mature until every spice and flavour was a harmony. My grandmother had once told me of a pickle, a lime and ginger pickle, which her great-grandmother had made and left to settle for a hundred years. 'For a hundred years the women in our family brought the pickle out in the morning to put in the sun, and then in the evenings they took it in again and left it in the kitchen. It had become a sacred chore, one they did without questioning or complaining. They had got so used to it that no one ever thought of eating the pickle.' This was clearly an exaggeration, but I listened spell-bound as always, while Ammi dipped dexterously into her silver pan box for a folded betel leaf.

'Nobody ever thought of eating that lemon and ginger pickle because it had been saved up for so long. It had become like a medicine—like an elixir, you could say. Anything that outlives its appointed span of years has achieved success, and over a hundred years that pickle certainly had! We were all saving it up for something; we didn't quite know what.

'And then, one day, the need arose to use it,' my Ammi continued. 'We had always known that this pickle was destined either for a great celebration or a medical emergency. Well, when your Mamoojan, my youngest brother who I treated like a son, was just seven, he fell very ill. He wouldn't eat any food, he wouldn't drink any water and he was wasting away before my eyes. I had already lost four children; four pretty young girls had died before your mother decided to live on and torment me. Now he was ill, this son who was not my son, and I had to do something. The jar of pickles was opened. That afternoon, when we finally got down to removing the lid from the bottle, all of us gathered in the courtyard under the mango tree and inhaled the scent of lemon. It was not an ordinary glass bottle, my dear . . . It was a special china boyam that had been ordered only for that pickle. Your uncle had the first spoon. At first he puckered his little lips because of the sour taste, and then he began smiling. He smiled, and then he laughed. His appetite returned and he was well again!

'What happened then, Ammi?' I had asked. It had seemed like a disappointingly tame end to an exciting story.

'What happened?' What happened indeed! I decided that, now that we had opened it, it was time to eat the pickle.

There is a cycle to saving things, to preserving them, and then to devouring them, letting them go. For the next few days, everybody in our household ate from the china boyam. They ate the pickle with relish and abandon. Neighbours, and even strangers, came to the door to ask of the hundred-year-old pickle. While we still had it, we refused nobody. Perhaps those blessings I got from grateful strangers were what carried us through our days of adversity!'

'What happened then, Ammi,' I had persisted, sitting on her lap, playing with the soft folds of her sari.

'What happened indeed! Your Mamoojan had no sense, no discretion, even less than your mother! He got worked up about some minor incident, a matter of no consequence; I've even forgotten what it was. The lemon pickle had saved his life once, but it hadn't cured him of the consequences of his own stupidity. He decided to end his life, to hang himself from the mango tree, the same mango tree in the courtyard in whose shade we had first opened the jar of pickle. Well, he died, and here I am, still alive, and quite happy to tell you the story.'

I watched a large tear balance itself on the edge of her eye, and her hand moved to wipe it away with her sari pallav. As I examined my glass jar of red pickles I remembered the story again. I missed my grandmother, but she was there with me, in the act of pickling and the act of remembering and the act of surviving.

THIRTY-EIGHT

One day Phoolwati decided to celebrate her birthday. As she had no idea when she had been born, the decision was essentially an arbitary one. That night we settled down to a little party, just the two of us. Sundar was away on his important business and Phoolwati was overjoyed to have me to herself. We gorged ourselves on halva and puri and pakodas and Phoolwati's famous parathas and other deep-fried and fattening food. Phoolwati kept plying me with more, urging me to 'eat for two'. As Sundar was away, we had the house to ourselves. We wandered from room to room, admiring the opulent decor and congratulating ourselves on our good taste. After the squalid rooms in Shiv Mohan's house, I found the extravagant colours and textures Phoolwati had employed uplifting and exhilarating. I felt as though a stone had been lifted from my heart and softly fondled my belly, blessing the baby within.

We pored through the snapshots of the wedding, taken by Sundar's friend. There was a group photograph of the band, where Mr Shiv Mohan's fly was unzipped for posterity. We both found this unbearably funny, and collapsed on to the sofas in uncontrollable laughter.

We settled down to a game of cards. We tried rummy and coatpiece and flash, but I was such an inexperienced gambler that Phoolwati got bored of explaining the difference between a queen of hearts and a queen of diamonds to me.

We decided to watch a film on the video. It was an old Hindi tear-jerker. The hero was a bandit with a heart of gold. 'Just like my Sundar, don't you think,' Phoolwati cooed.

That set me thinking about Kalki, and I was unusually pensive. Phoolwati sensed my change of mood and misconstrued the reason behind it.

'Missing your bandwallah again?' she asked crudely. 'That Kalki must be some man!'

Everything about Phoolwati looked suddenly vulgar, obese and offensive. I told her so, but she was not unduly hurt. 'Just like any newly wed,' she said cheerfully. 'I was the same in the beginning, even with that Shambhu.

'And that reminds me,' she continued. 'Your money is safe here. Remember that it is always available to you.'

Then she began talking about Roxanne's will. Phoolwati was of the insistent opinion that I was not to let Cyrus and Mr Lamba walk away with everything. 'After all, your madam was not a child, though God knows she behaved like one. If she left you her money she must have had some reason for it,' she said, in the stubborn reproachful tone which I knew would brook no retreat.

Phoolwati wanted me to sign a document granting power of attorney to a lawyer whom Sundar knew, allowing him the legal right to proceed on my behalf. I trusted Phoolwati implicitly. To some extent I trusted Sundar as well, but this was too delicate a matter to be left to his rough dealings. 'I'll have to consider it,' I said.

She looked at me thoughtfully. 'So you're growing up, Gudiya Rani,' she murmured, as though not entirely pleased by this development.

We settled down to watch another film. Phoolwati fortified herself with cough syrup, while I feasted on a box of pista burfi which she had specially sent for to celebrate her birthday.

The next morning, I awoke late to find Sundar Pahalwan polishing off a substantial breakfast of several stuffed parathas and a brimming glass of lassi. He looked preoccupied, even worried, and for the first time in my life I saw him snap at Phoolwati.

In spite of my own experiences with Kalki, I was a little disconcerted by this show of temper and Phoolwati's placid acceptance of it.

I visited Pandit Kailash Shastry at the mandir. The Shiva shrine that Sundar and Phoolwati had constructed was now complete, as were the modifications which the pandit had effected in strict accordance with the principles of Vastu Shastra. The temple seemed strange without any bags of cement or steel girders scattered around. I suddenly remembered the slab of green marble my Ammi had purloined from the building site so many years ago. I searched for it through the temple premises, but it was nowhere in sight. There was a length of dark-coloured stone, smeared with oil and vermilion, looking very old indeed, but it was not the green-veined marble upon which we had laid the foundations of our temple.

The pandit was full of brisk energy, busily conducting prayers for the morning contingent of devotees. Two acolytes, of impeccable Brahminical stock, replete with shaven heads and chotis, were on hand to assist him.

Panditji offered to read my hand, but I refused. There was nothing about my future I any longer wanted to know about. I was ready for whatever came my way. But Kailash Shastry couldn't help himself. 'You will have a daughter,' he said, 'and she will bring great good luck to her father.'

I was intrigued in spite of myself. Perhaps Kalki would become a famous film star! He might even win a lottery! A brief chimera of a rich, reformed, house-broken Kalki floated tantalizingly before me. It took all of my self-control to suppress my natural curiosity and refrain from asking him any further questions.

The pandit's prognostications had put me in such a positive state of mind that I decided to spend the afternoon at a beauty parlour. A number of such establishments had mushroomed in our locality, and the 'Lovely Beauty Hut' had been emphatically recommended by Phoolwati, who was by now hopelessly addicted to the joys of cream-massage and shampoo and blow-dry. I looked into the many mirrors that crowded the room. I could barely recognize myself. I imagined I saw many faces staring back. Which of them was me? The reflected images echoed the question through the wilderness of mirrors, until the beautician broke into my reverie, asking what shade of nail polish I wanted to use. I settled on Midnight Magic, a frosty magenta lacquer. After I had been kneaded and pounded with cream and unguents, and my hair oiled and de-oiled and artfully styled into a cascade of flowing curls, I returned to Phoolwati's house.

We watched yet another Hindi film on television, and sat around amicably until Sundar returned. Remembering his foul mood of the morning, I kept tactfully out of the way. He was drunk at night, shouting and slurring and knocking about the house. The sweet-sick smell of country liquor flooded the rooms. I found it impossible to sleep and tossed and turned nervously in bed all night.

Perhaps because I had slept so late, I did not awake until ten the next morning. Changing out of my flimsy night-clothes, I hurried out to look for Phoolwati. She was standing at the front door haranguing the municipal sweeperess for her incompetence.

A mountain of garbage had piled up on the street outside the entrance, and the sweeperess was insisting that, as theirs was an unauthorized construction, she was entitled to a private salary from Phoolwati for cleaning it.

Sundar sauntered out demanding to know what the matter was. I saw his huge frame outlined against the door, shutting out the harsh sunlight, just as I had seen him the first time he had come to our hut to demand his haftha from my Ammi.

He stepped out of the house. There was a moment's silence, for even the sweepers knew better than to argue with Sundar Pahalwan. As she was sullenly murmuring her apologies, the sharp retort of a machine-gun rang out, shattering the morning calm.

I ran out of the house. The smell of garbage clung to the air. I saw Sundar stagger a few steps, and then he slumped and fell down. Still the unknown sniper did not stop.

Sundar was inescapably dead. His head rested on a chewed-up banana, and a sheaf of torn-up lottery-tickets fluttered before his lifeless eyes.

Phoolwati did not scream or cry out or weep or respond in any of the ways I might have expected. Instead, quietly, and with great dignity, she slowly dragged Sundar's body back into the house. Then she sat down beside him and began systematically breaking her green glass bangles on the cold marble floor.

'Should I call the police?' I asked wildly. 'Or the ambulance?'

'The police will turn up anyway,' Phoolwati replied wearily. Sundar's men arrived and took charge of matters. They did not call the police or the ambulance, but began methodically roughing up the entire neighbourhood, slapping and threatening even the women and children on the street, warning them not to talk too much to the authorities, searching their houses and seeking out the unknown assassin.

When the police arrived they were not much gentler. They interrogated Phoolwati mercilessly and settled themselves on her plush new sofas like an occupying force. A press photographer also arrived, and he took a picture of the grieving widow. The policemen kept demanding tea, and there was nobody to make it but me.

Later, I doped Phoolwati with vast quantities of cough syrup. The funeral was a grand affair, with gangsters and hoodlums from all over Delhi turning up in full strength. Several politicians and important people were also to be seen.

The obituary in the papers was drafted by Phoolwati and Pandit Kailash Shastry. It quoted a quite irrelevant text from the Geeta. At first we couldn't locate an appropriate picture of Sundar, until I remembered my wedding photographs. Phoolwati insisted on a quarter page obituary, and Sundar's portrait, framed in black, stared at us from all the papers the next day.

Pandit Kailash Shastry took over the task of consoling Phoolwati. He set about rationalizing the tragedy by concluding, after the event, that it had been inevitable. 'A weak moon, Mars in the tenth,' he murmured comfortingly. 'Saturn by Ketu aspected by Mars—that clearly indicates death by weapons.' He had known all along that Sundar Pahalwan's days in this world were numbered, there was a conjunction of planets and so on. He so distracted Phoolwati with ceremony and ritual that she soon recovered and was her normal self again.

THIRTY-NINE

Kalki did not write to me from Bombay. I never heard from him again. Phoolwati thought she glimpsed him in a Hindi film—he was one of the extras in a dance sequence. We saw the film—it was called *Dil Diwana Hai*—innumerable times, in cinema halls, and at home on the video, but we could never really be sure.

'If Sundar were alive he would have traced that Kalki to the gates of hell!' Phoolwati said tragically. I was afraid she would start weeping, something she had become increasingly prone to, but she pulled herself together.

'Anyway, you are probably better off without him,' she continued pragmatically. 'And I would have been left all alone if both of you weren't there for me. Perhaps it's for the best.'

We live together, Phoolwati, Mallika and me. Mallika is now two years old, and looks amazingly like my Ammi. Lila insists that it is a case of reincarnation and would have begun subjecting my little daughter to ritual worship had not the pandit and Phoolwati emphatically interceded.

Phoolwati saved my life a few months ago. We were strolling through the narrow streets of Chandni Chowk, where we had gone to buy silver payals for Mallika, when an enraged cow began charging directly towards me. I had Mallika in my arms. Phoolwati pushed us out of the way and stood before the maddened creature, warding it off with her enormous synthetic leather handbag. The cow was not to be deterred and gored her in the midriff.

Phoolwati had to be taken to the emergency ward, where she was given seven stitches across her stomach. She was heroic about it, insisting that, with her weight, she had fat and flesh to spare. Her belly, swathed in bandages, made a strange sight under her sari pallav and afforded Mallika great amusement.

On the whole, Phoolwati has coped admirably with Sundar's death. 'Nothing good ever lasts very long,' she says often, with fatalistic certainty.

Mrs Dubash staged a miraculous recovery, confounding the doctors and her son-in-law. The question of Roxanne Lamba's inheritance, whether pertaining to Mr Lamba, Cyrus, St. Jude's or me, is for the moment again academic, rendered invalid by the will of that resilient old woman.

The recording rights to the tapes of Ammi's bhajans have been bought by a prominent music company. The life of the temple flourishes, and, according to Phoolwati, even the lepers have built up substantial savings accounts in the local banks.

All kinds of construction—small shrines, a boundary wall, a piau, have crowded around the contours of my peepul tree. It has lost none of its mystery, but it has become somehow domesticated, tamed, habituated. Many times, as the day fades and the evening shadows fall, I find my daughter Mallika at play under its sheltering branches. I am certain then that my friends and familiars are watching over her. I glance up, involuntarily, but they no longer recall themselves, although I can often hear a familiar sigh or catch the fragment of a familiar song from the rustle of the gentle green leaves.

Maria Smetacek, Pandit Kailash Shastry's German disciple, has returned to India. Together they plan to update *Raman's Ninety-year Ephemeris*. They talk interminably of sidereal time, the retrograde movement of planets and the balance of dashas at birth in an oriental horoscope. It is a marriage of true minds. The pandit is not a sanyasi, only a brahmachari—he has not yet formally renounced the world. According to Phoolwati, it is certain they will tie the knot—if, that is, they are not already secretly married.

Once in a while, I take out my single remaining gold sovereign and stare at the noble profile of Emperor Jehangir and his consort Noorjehan. As I hold the coin in my hand, I try to conjure up the life in the old haveli with the hundred-and-thirty rooms, the laughter and gaiety and chandeliers and silver chalices of wine overflowing onto a flowered Persian carpet.

Sometimes I go through the photographs of my marriage—the assembled band and Kalki in his dark suit. It all seems far away and unreal. In actual fact, I have all but forgotten him.

When enough time passes, and the dust settles on those troubled memories, perhaps I shall be able to embellish them with a veil of fabulism and mystery. Rendering the past acceptable, if not accountable, is a talent I inherited from my Ammi.

It is easy to live in the present. Life in Phoolwati's house—poetically called 'The Ashiana'—has a soothing sameness in its rhythm. Phoolwati is invariably gentle with Mallika and me. I have seen her looking at me speculatively, assessing for damage, but she wisely keeps her silence.

I often dream about my mother, but she is elusive even there. Grandmother is dead, Roxanne is dead, Sundar is dead. Even Kalki is gone, but the end of the world is nowhere in sight.